ONLINE

MADELEINE TAYLOR

Edited by Claire Jarrett

Cover design by Meg Sayers

1

The green light flashes on and her picture appears. My reaction is always the same; a strange sense of excitement deep in my core that makes me restless and desperate for her attention. We're in different time zones and far apart, with me living in Los Angeles and her life being in Quebec, but we always seem to be online at the same time. I don't know if her name or her profile picture are real but mine are. I only use my first name, Valerie, and she goes by Syd.

If the profile picture is indeed real and recent, Syd looks to be in her late thirties. She has dark, pixie-cut hair and the most spectacular light blue eyes. I always thought they were colored lenses—the shade so startlingly blue—before she assured me, during one of our rare non-book related talks when it was just us in the book club's forum, that they were real. Her high cheekbones and defined jawline give off a European vibe, but the scant information I could find on her profile tells me she's Canadian.

My profile picture is fairly recent. It was taken after my long and painful divorce on a celebratory night out, and I look as happy as I felt that evening—finally free from the man who cheated on me for years. Now single, Ellen, my best friend, decided it was the perfect time for me to start online dating and told me I needed a good picture for that. It's only a headshot, just like hers. My long dark hair is pulled up into a topknot and I'm wearing a black turtleneck and only a little make up, as my dark eyes and eyebrows don't require much. Being half Hawaiian, I have my mother's exotic features, tanned skin and heart-shaped face, and after going through a phase of bleaching my hair in my twenties, the color is natural again.

Our book club consists of twenty members from all over the world, all of us a mixture of ages and with very little in common apart from one thing: we all love to read lesbian erotica. It's been my guilty pleasure ever since I bought the wrong book online by accident, mistaking my purchase for something with the same title. I did think the cover of *The Red Room* looked a little different from the type of book I usually buy, but tired and grumpy after waiting up for my husband, who didn't come home that night, I purchased it without thinking. I remember laughing to myself when it arrived on my screen, noticing the explicit cover and that the author was someone called Sadie London instead of Mark Finsburgh. One look and it was patently obvious it had nothing to do with anger management coaching on the work floor. Scanning through it, I got curious and like a woman starved of attention started reading it. *The Red Room* soon woke up parts of my body I'd neglected for years and since that day, I've been reading one lesbian erotica book after another, and still can't seem to get enough of them.

No one knows this hidden side of me, apart from the nineteen other members of my book club. The website isn't very well known, and the chat element is closed, so I feel safe to discuss my newfound passion with likeminded enthusiasts. The main reason I keep coming back religiously each night though, is Syd.

Of course, I've thought long and hard about my fascination with her. She's attractive—again, if her profile picture is real—but there's also something personal in the way she communicates with me and it makes me feel special. I know that sounds sad, but I haven't exactly been dating much, too consumed with reading after work and frankly right now, I'd take lesbian erotica over a date with a man any day.

I'm not even sure if I'm still into men as I clearly don't have much interest in them. When I was still married our sex life wasn't exactly sizzling, and even before things started going south between us, I never enjoyed having sex as much as my friends claimed they did. Perhaps that's why I like reading about good sex instead because, contrary to the real deal, it turns me on.

'*Valerie.*'

Syd typing my name is enough to make my pulse race. '*Syd ,*' I reply.

'*It seems like it's just us again. Did you finish the book?*'

'*Yes. In one day. I liked it. Well written and very hot. Did you?*'

'*I did. Cherry reminded me of you, in a way.*'

I frown, wondering how she came to that conclusion, because honestly Cherry, the protagonist in our latest book club read, reminded me of myself too. '*Why?*' I ask.

'*Not sure. The bad-ass job, maybe, and you seem to use the same language. Her description fits your profile picture too, so my mind just went there...*'

It's not so much what she types, but the three dots at the end that make me take in a quick breath. We're not supposed to discuss anything other than the books we read in the group, so I phrase my reply carefully, the way we always do when we want to find out more about each other.

By now, I know she's a tattoo artist and that she's into running. In return, I told her I work as a CFO for a large electronics company and that I'm a wine enthusiast but that's about it.

'I guess I could relate to her because of her job. Maybe that's why I liked it so much. I'm not exactly a blonde bombshell, though.'

'I'll have to disagree with that. Blonde, maybe not. A bombshell, most certainly.'

The comment makes me blush, and I look around, even though I know there's no one left in the office. It's 8 pm and most of my team members leave before seven, but because I had a late meeting and didn't want to risk missing my precious half hour with her, I got back behind my desk in my corner office afterward, swapping my work phone for my private one. *'Well, thank you,'* is all I can think of to say. Syd's been on my mind a lot lately, and although I feel a little foolish for being so pre-occupied with someone who I don't even know is real, it's also been nice to have something to fantasize about again. Being an avid reader of lesbian erotica herself, I know there's a good chance Syd is gay, and it's a flattering thought that a beautiful woman might be into me.

I wait for a reply, and then it happens. I've been imagining this moment many times late at night in bed, when I can't sleep and can't stop thinking of her. Against all club rules, she sends me her personal email address and adds: *'I'd like to continue this conversation in private'*, before going offline.

I stare at it for a moment, not quite believing what she's just done, then quickly copy it into my contacts before the mediator has the chance to remove it. We might get suspended for this, but I don't care. My heart is beating steadily in my chest as I read her name in the email address. *Sydney Heller.* I don't know why it feels like such a big deal to know her surname, but suddenly, nothing seems more important than sending her an email. I scan the office again and contemplate doing it here, but unsure of how long I'll be waiting for her reply, I close my laptop and pack my bag instead. The traffic in LA will be fine at this time of night and I can be home in half an hour.

2

'*Hi Syd,*' I type when I'm sitting on the couch after a shower. Reluctant to waste time driving around in search of food, I've settled for a glass of red wine and the leftovers of last night's Thai take-out. I'm not hungry in the slightest, my nerves suppressing my appetite, but I force myself to eat something so I'm not drinking on an empty stomach. How do I continue? In theory, this should be easier than communicating face to face or in a group where everyone can see what we're writing, but it's not. I feel feverishly warm and open my robe a little, fanning my face with a magazine from the table.

Despite my reputation as a wild child when I was younger, sending this email seems like a reckless thing to do. Knowing she'll be flirting with me when our exchange starts, my brain begins searching for something witty or intelligent to say, but nothing springs to mind—it's all a blank—my mind suddenly void. What's wrong with me? I lead a team of thirty in my day to day role and have no problem confidently consulting some of the most powerful people in my industry. In meetings or discussions, I'm always one step ahead of everyone else, yet sending a simple email seems terribly complicated right now. I curse when I almost drop my phone, and the two-word email is sent by accident in a clumsy scramble to catch it.

"Fuck, fuck, fuck!" The last of the three 'fucks' comes out as a cry when on top of everything, I spill wine over my silk robe, leaving a red stain on the delicate off-white fabric. Irritated, I quickly grab a dish towel to wipe myself off as a ping indicates a reply.

'Hey, Valerie. I must say, you've been on my mind a lot lately. Is your profile picture real? You look beautiful.'

I feel flushed at her message and a twitch stronger than I've felt in years shoots between my thighs. The way my body reacts to her compliment surprises me. Still unable to think of anything amusing, I start typing the first thing that comes to mind.

'Yes, it's real. What about yours?' My fingers tremble as I continue. *'You're very attractive yourself.'*

Her reply again, is prompt. *'Yes, it's me. See pic attached. What are you doing right now?'* Almost choking with anticipation, I open the attachment, not sure whether to expect a dick pic as a result of being catfished by some cruel prankster or an actual picture of Syd. Relief washes over me when I see it's an image of her. It looks like it's been taken with a selfie stick, because I can see most of her. She's sitting on a bed holding a bottle of beer. One of her arms is entirely covered in tattoos, and she's wearing a white tank top and jeans, smiling into the camera, her piercing light blue eyes focused on the lens. She looks strong and toned, with small breasts and a slight curve at her hips. It's the first time I've ever stared at a woman's body like this and I can't help but wonder what she would look like naked.

'Nice picture. I'm on the couch, just got home.'

'*Perfect. I'm at home now too, and bored. I need you to distract me.*'

A shiver runs through me as I reply. Are we really doing this? '*Happy to help. What can I do for you?*'

'*Well for starters, where's my picture? I need proof too.*'

I smile and take a selfie, wishing I'd freshened up before I started this. Cringing as I look at the wine stain splashed over my left breast, I send it anyway, not wanting her to think I'm trying too hard. '*Here's your proof.*'

'*Cute. I like it . What happened to your robe?*'

'*I spilled wine.*' Typing the words, I remember the still half-full glass on the coffee table and take a long drink, then fill it up again. Liquid courage is exactly what I need right now. This time, the reply doesn't come straight away and I start to worry if my disheveled appearance in the picture has put her off. It wasn't dissimilar from my profile picture, apart from my hair, which is down now but perhaps I should have rethought the robe? Finally, she gets back to me and my eyes widen as I read her message.

'*It looks wet. Maybe you should take it off.*'

Initially, I'm shocked by her directness but deep down, it also arouses me. I should have seen this coming, of course. No one starts a flirty exchange without expecting it to turn sexy. I could always tell her I've taken it off, she can't see me after all. But something makes me want to do it, and so I slide the silky fabric off my shoulders, leaving me in the pastel pink lace bra I've been wearing all day. '*It's off.*'

'*I'm going to need proof of that too, I'm afraid.*'

I laugh and shake my head. '*Why would I send a half-naked picture of myself to a stranger? You could do anything with it.*'

'*But I won't. I promise I won't, so just send me the picture.*'

I bite my lip, contemplating her request while heat

spreads between my thighs. It's so not me, but then neither is being a member of a lesbian erotica book club. Knowing I'll give in—because my body really, really wants this—I take another sip of wine so I can blame it on the alcohol if my picture ends up online. *'You'd better keep this to yourself, Syd,'* I type, then take another picture of me in my bra. I'm not smiling in this one, but as I narrow my eyes and study myself, I notice I look aroused. It may not be obvious to her, as she doesn't know me, but my own impassioned expression astounds me. My lips are parted, my eyes darker than normal and there's even a hint of fear in them that could easily be mistaken for vulnerability, or shyness. Still, I send it and try not to think of the potential consequences of my irrational behavior.

'Thank you. That's very sexy... How about we play a game? It's called I tell you what to do and you obey.'

I chuckle at her audacity and note that subtlety is not her strong point. *'That doesn't sound like a fair game to me.'*

'Maybe not, but it could be fun.' She ends her message with a wink emoji. While I take my time contemplating her indecent proposal—wondering how I should reply—another email comes in. *'Are you still there?'*

'Yes, I'm here,' I type with trembling fingers.

'Good. Because I want you to slide your hand into your bra. Feel your nipples harden under your touch. Roll them between your fingers and pinch them.'

I gasp as my eyes scan her message. I'm not used to people telling me what to do and she's unapologetically bold and direct. I quickly type back.

'Oh, we've started now, have we? I don't remember agreeing to this.'

'Just do as I say, and you'll be rewarded. I promise.'

Part of me is afraid, but part of me also likes her

demanding tone. If I'm doing anything on a Monday night, it might as well be this, and I surprise myself by following her command. My fingers skim my already hard nipples, the tips of which rose to attention the moment her first email came in. A small gasp escapes me as I pinch them, and my pussy twitches with arousal.

'*It feels good,*' I type with one hand.

'*I know it does. Now take off your bra and show me those nipples. I want to imagine my lips on them.*'

My shaking hand covers my mouth and I stare at the screen for a long moment. This is getting out of hand, but by now I'm so turned on that I actually want to continue. I unclasp my bra at the back and let it fall off my shoulders, shivering at the breeze that blows in through the sliding glass doors. Cropping the picture I've hastily taken, I make sure only the bottom half of my face is in it so I can always deny that it's me. Not bothering with a caption, I send it and again, it seems to take forever before she gets back to me.

'*Fuck. You are so hot.*'

I smile and can feel myself blushing because it's been a long time since someone has said that to me. '*Where's my topless picture?*' I daringly request.

'*Next time. I have to go. Send me your Messenger info, it's much easier.*'

'*What's in it for me?*' I ask, suddenly kicking myself for sending semi-racy pictures of myself to a woman I don't know. What if she sells them? What if she blackmails me? For someone in my position, I can't risk having my reputation tainted.

'*You'll find out soon enough. Expect a package at work tomorrow. Your reward.*'

Adrenaline floods my system, and I'm feeling even more worried now. '*How do you know where I work?*'

'*Your email address, smart-ass .*' Straight after, another email follows. '*Bye. X*'

"Damn it," I say out loud. Why am I not thinking clearly this evening? Or rather, why am I not thinking at all? I rarely send private emails, and I realize I've used my work account which is connected to my personal devices too, without thinking. I immediately delete the emails and pictures, then down the rest of my wine. I'm not sure if I'm relieved or disappointed that she's gone because, despite my concerns, I'm still incredibly turned on. Wishing I'd kept the picture she sent me, I slide my hand into my panties and gasp at how sensitive I am. Slowly, I trace two fingers up and down my flesh, moaning as I roll my hips. The need for release is strong and I move my fingers faster, almost frantically. It's been too long, and my clit is throbbing as I circle it, my release loud as I cry out when my much-needed orgasm washes over me.

Basking in blissful relaxation, I stare up at the ceiling and realize I need more of this, more of her. I love the way she talks to me, the way she makes no excuses and simply tells me what she wants. Maybe I should just go with it, because it seems that the licentious fantasies I've had during my time in the book club are finally coming true...

3

"Thank you, that will be all." I close my laptop and gather my paperwork from the enormous oval table in the boardroom. My staff is leaving for lunch after our monthly briefing and I'm headed for the mail room. During our meeting, a message from the mail room supervisor came in, letting me know there was a parcel for me. It was hard to concentrate on my presentation —knowing it might be Syd's package—and the two hours felt like they would never end.

Walking toward the elevators, I give a polite nod to a couple of co-workers and smile at the janitor I often talk to at night, when we're the last ones left in the office. Our enormous office building is spacious and decorated in neutral colors, the sleek and modern design making it feel like a clinic at times. I don't mind that; I like no-nonsense and dress accordingly. My pantsuits that are custom-made for my petite, but curvy body are like a uniform to me. I wear them to work every single day; a fitted black blazer that accentuates my slim waist, black palazzo pants, high heels and a black sleeveless turtleneck. It's always a little on the chilly side here, in summer as well as in winter, and being uncomfortable is a waste of time.

A text message from my friend Ellen comes in, asking me if I want to go for dinner tonight. For a moment, the idea seems great, but then I remember last night's exchange, and I change my mind, replying that I'm busy. I still need to send Syd my Messenger details, but I want to see what's in the parcel first.

"What have you got for me, Pete?" I ask the mail room supervisor. Normally, I'd send my assistant to pick it up, but I'm a little apprehensive about what the packaging will look like and I don't want her to make assumptions or ask questions. I'm relieved when Pete presents me with a neutral black box, laced with a pink ribbon that is tied into a perfect bow on the top. Thankfully, there's no card and no logo on the box.

"It was hand-delivered this morning," Pete says. "By a pretty lady in a pink delivery truck. I don't remember the name of the company. Naughty something..." He frowns, digging through his memory, and I cringe.

"Right, thank you. It's probably just some marketing material addressed to the wrong department. I'll make sure it gets to the right person." My cheeks burn with heat, and I rush out of the mail room and into the nearest restrooms, where I sit down on a toilet seat and take a deep breath. After staring at the box for a moment, I pull at the ribbon, releasing it, then open the lid. Black satin fabric surrounds a small, pink device, along with a card that says: *'Don't use this until I tell you to.'*

It's a vibrator, and from the looks of it, it's an expensive one. I take it out of the box and study the streamlined silicone toy. Even though I don't have any experience with vibrators—in fact I don't think I've ever seen one up close—

I appreciate the design. It appears clever and uncomplicated, but above all, it looks intriguing. The bent oval shape fits perfectly in my hand and when I press the single ridged circle on the top, it starts buzzing. The feeling of it makes me quiver and the temptation to try it right now is strong, but looking down at the card again, I switch it off and put it back in the box. *Tonight*, I tell myself. Right now, I need to hide this box and grab a coffee before my next meeting starts.

I'm not taking much in from the planning meeting with the wearables marketing manager who is pitching his estimated budgets to me. There are another handful of people in the room but they're really just here as a formality as, ultimately, it's my decision how much he's allocated for the coming year. I should pay close attention as this is important but just before we started, I emailed Syd my Messenger details and now my phone is buzzing. Moving my phone to my lap under the table, I open the message.

'*Did you get my present?*'

I reply. '*Yes. It's a little much and a little soon, don't you think?*'

'*Don't fool yourself, I know what you want. We've been discussing erotica books for months and I know you're into this. You also seemed to be into me last night. So... do you like it?*'

'*Yes, I do. Thank you.*' I realize then that she does in fact know what I want. Admitting I like a certain book is basically the same as revealing my fantasies. The second book I read by Sadie London springs to mind. It was about the owner of a sex store who tried out various toys on her clients. Clearly recalling telling the other members of the club it was my favorite book, and that I'm working my way through all of the author's books now, I think she's drawing from it, and knowing she remembers that makes me smile. The marketing manager smiles too, hopeful that my silly grin means I'm on board with his proposition. I try to relax my face and pretend to listen while shooting another quick glance at my phone when it vibrates again.

'*Is your pussy shaven?*' I gasp at the question, and suddenly, six pairs of eyes are focused on me. I shouldn't be doing this here. My company is paying me a small fortune to make big decisions and I'm sexting in the middle of a meeting. Breaking into a coughing fit, I pretend to have a sore throat. It seems to do the trick, as everyone waits for me to finish clearing my throat, before turning back to the presenter, who is only on slide seven of which I know to be a forty-slide pitch. Despite my fleeting lapse in concentration, I don't panic. I've read the presentation through beforehand, so at least I won't be entirely clueless by the end of this. The pull to continue the exchange with Syd is strong, and now that I've had some time to get used to the idea—that I'm indecently messaging a woman—I can't seem to make myself stop.

My fingers move silently under the table. '*Trimmed,*' I lie, knowing I haven't bothered with too much personal grooming since I last stopped sleeping with my ex-husband three years ago. Now I regret that I didn't because who knows what will happen tonight?

'*Hmm...*' A couple of seconds pass before another message comes in. '*I want you to shave yourself first. All of it. It will be much more intense if you do. Trust me.*' There's another pause before she writes: '*Have to go, talk to you later.*' She closes the message with her usual wink emoji, then leaves the chat.

I'm so turned on by her request that I have to push my

chair back and cross my legs in an attempt to sooth the agonizing tingle between my thighs. Scrolling through my phone, I look up the number for the beauty parlor I always book when I have a last-minute business trip. If I'm doing this I might as well do it right and I've decided I'm going to get myself waxed.

4

I settle down on the couch after subjecting myself to what can only be described as the worst pain in my life. I won't claim it has anything on childbirth, because I don't have children, but it was still pretty intolerable. I don't regret it though, as the drive home was sensational. It felt like everything down there was ultra-sensitive, and even just shifting in the leather driver's seat aroused me. When I came home, I undressed and studied myself in the mirror, noting it was strange and shockingly confrontational to see myself like that. Naked, but really, really naked. Now that I'm sitting back after a long shower, I can't seem to stop touching myself. My pussy is so soft, and my fingers alone feel divine on my silky skin as I stroke myself.

Syd's present is next to me on the coffee table, still in the box. My assistant had my favorite robe dry-cleaned today and I'm wearing it again, the faint traces of red wine barely visible anymore. I'm naked underneath the robe, prepared for anything, and for the first time in years, I'm feeling desirable. I want to contact her, but this whole woman thing is new to me and, although I've been unable to think of anything else all day, I'm a little apprehensive. Gathering my courage over an impressive measure of scotch, I send her a message. *'I'm home. What are you doing?'*

'Waiting for you to get home,' she answers immediately.

'Not working?' I ask, as she told me her tattoo parlor is open at random times, to suit both herself and her customers.

'Not today. Today is for inspiration.'

'Right...' I send, then add: *'What does that mean?'*

'Means I'm talking to you. You inspire me.'

A grin spreads across my face because, as sad as it sounds, it's one of the nicest things someone has ever said to me—even if she does have ulterior motives that by now, I don't mind in the slightest. Her profile picture is a different one on Messenger, another headshot with a wide smile and again, those amazing pale blue eyes staring right at me as if she's seducing me to look at her. *'I'm glad I inspire you. Now, where's my picture?'*

The picture she sends me shortly after appears to have been taken in her bedroom, but I can't be too sure as I can only see the top part of her body, from her waist up. It's enough to make me squirm, though. She's lying down, looking up at the camera with a mischievous grin on her face. Her white shirt is open and, for my viewing pleasure, she's wearing nothing underneath. I zoom in on her small breasts with erect nipples, and I want to touch them so badly, I groan to myself. The urge to touch a woman is not something I'm familiar with, but the agonizing ache in my core tells me I might die if I don't.

'You're beautiful,' I find myself typing.

'Thank you. Whatever you're wearing, take it off and send me a picture. I've been waiting to see you all day.'

I open my robe and this time, without hesitation, take a

picture from the waist up. Whatever leverage she's got on me, I have it on her too, now.

'I love your breasts, can't stop fantasizing about them. So full and perky. Where's the rest?'

'Are you serious?' I ask.

'Yes. I want to see what my present will be pressed against.'

Fuck. I should have expected this after her audacious request this afternoon. With a trembling hand, I take another picture, the camera pointing down my body. One leg is bent, the other stretched out in front of me. The photo is subtle, yet it's clear what I've been doing today. *'Like this?'*

'Fuck, yes. You're turning me on, Valerie.'

'It hurt,' I reply with a crying emoji.

'And now?'

'Now it feels great. So sensitive...'

'I like that.' Then she writes: *'Pick up my present. You haven't tried it yet, have you?'*

'No, I haven't. You told me not to.' I take out the vibrator and take a picture of it in my hand. I'm so wet and swollen and the all-consuming urge to push it between my legs is almost killing me. Still, I don't act on this impulse. I want her to tell me when.

'Good. Now spread your legs and place the tip against your clit. Turn it on. The harder you press down, the harder it will vibrate.'

I do as she says, gasping when I switch it on. *Jesus.* It feels so incredibly good, and when I push it tighter against me, the force increases, almost launching me off the couch. Why have I never tried this before? It's hard to type with the currents of pleasure pulsing through me. *'It feels so incredibly good...'* I buck my hips, seeking the release I know will come very soon. *'I'm going to come.'*

'No!' She immediately replies. *'Remove it. Now.'*

'*Why?*' My frustration and need to climax almost make me ignore her, but I do as she commands.

'*Trust me. You'll thank me in a little while. I'm going to make you come harder than you ever have, and I'm not even going to be there. Now wait one minute.*'

My chest is heaving up and down, my heartrate through the roof. I'm so aroused that I can't even move my legs, knowing any sudden movement will make me explode. My robe is open, one leg draped over the backrest of the couch, my louche pose a far cry from the powerful woman I was portraying in the boardroom this afternoon. Now she's the one giving out orders and it seems like I'm more than happy to follow them. This woman is driving me insane and I'm shocked at how submissive I've become. She's been on my mind all day and even messaging with her now doesn't nearly seem enough to tamp down my desires.

'*Now,*' she orders me, and I place the vibrator back against my throbbing clit.

"Fuck!" I cry out, trying to type, but failing.

'*Stop.*'

Letting out a sigh of frustration as I balance on the edge, I reluctantly remove the vibrator again and lie so still that I don't even blink my eyes. Anything I do now will make me burst.

'*I can't tke this anyore.*' I'm unable to spell, my brain blurred by arousal of an alarming level.

'*I know. Just wait, one more time.*'

I stare at my screen, waiting for her to give me permission. I could cheat, of course, but it wouldn't be the same and, deep down, I like her to be in control.

'*Come,*' she finally types, and as I push the device hard against where I need it most, I cry out, losing myself in wave after wave of euphoric bliss. A sensation of intense pleasure keeps coming as white light flashes before my eyes, and my body explodes with such ferocity that I have trouble breathing. In shock by the fierceness of my orgasm, I'm a shaking mass of completion as I slump back against the pillows. Pulses continue to rip through me, and I almost forget she's there.

'*Fuck.*'

'*Was it good?*'

'*Yes.*' I laugh out loud as I type my response. '*Mind-blowing. Thank you. Best present ever.*'

'*You're welcome. Send me a picture of your face.*'

I take a picture and glance at the image before I send it. A satisfied grin is spread across my face and my eyes are hazy. My hair is tousled, like I've only just woken up, and the open robe has slipped off one shoulder, baring my collarbone. For the first time, I realize I look sexy.

'*You look amazing. So hot, like you've just been fucked.*' A beat passes, and then: '*I have to go now, talk tomorrow?*'

Before I get the chance to protest, she's offline. I sigh as I sit up and pull my legs underneath me, wishing she wouldn't just disappear like this. Is it her way of trying to keep me interested? Because if that's her strategy, there's no need for her to bother, as my interest is growing by the second, and tomorrow can't come soon enough. Blissfully relaxed, I close my robe and tell Alexa to play *O mio babbino caro* by *Puccini* while I finish my scotch.

5

———

"**Y**ou did what?!" My friend Ellen almost falls off her chair, laughing. We're having lunch at one of the latest hotspots downtown, sharing a bottle of wine over superfood salads. I've taken the afternoon off as I was unable to concentrate at work, memories of last night distracting me to the point where I couldn't even follow a simple conversation. Thankfully, I have Ellen to confide in because I really needed to tell someone about my online adventures.

Being a lady of leisure, Ellen is chilled, good fun and always available. We met through our husbands years ago but didn't really start bonding until we both got divorced. She's a funny, forty-five-year-old, voluptuous redhead who is now serial-dating much younger men, and she's been telling me how great it is, encouraging me to do the same.

"So let me get this straight," she continues, chuckling. "You joined a lesbian erotica book club, and you've been reading that stuff for months without telling me. Then, you correspond with this fellow reader online, and now she's sent you a vibrator resulting in you getting yourself waxed before having Messenger sex with her yesterday? Who are you and what have you done with my straight, divorced BFF Valerie?"

I feel myself blush and laugh too, because it sounds crazy when she says it like that. "I've been asking myself the same question. You know, you can't tell anyone about this," I add, giving her a warning look. I know she won't. Besides the fact that I trust her, we have no friends in common and in general, Ellen prefers to talk about Ellen.

"And? Was it good?" She narrows her eyes at me and shoots me a grin.

"Yes. Very." I poke into a piece of beetroot, then put my fork down. My appetite has vanished ever since Syd and I started whatever it is we're doing. "But it's also messing me up, big time. I can't eat or sleep or even think... I'm all over the place, Ellen."

Ellen rubs my hand over the table. "Hey, chill out, sweetheart, it's just a crush. Happens to me all the time these days." She hesitates. "So, are you into women now? I mean, you've been reading lesbian erotica and you seem blown away by this woman. You should see your face when you talk about her."

"I don't know," I say honestly. "But I know one thing: it was the best sex I've ever had, and she didn't even touch me. I can't begin to imagine what it would be like if we met." I shiver at that thought, imagining her hands on me, and I force myself to concentrate on Ellen in fear of spontaneously climaxing at the table.

"Oh my God, Valerie." Ellen fans her face with her hand. "You have it bad. And you're right; if it was that good without actual physical contact, I can see why you're going crazy here. So, what now?"

"No idea. We're talking again tonight."

"Talking, huh? That's what you call it?"

I take a sip of my wine and roll my eyes. "I have no idea what to call it. It's all so new to me. I do know I want more, though, and seeing her naked is all I can think of now."

"Is she on social media?" Ellen nods toward my phone. "Can I see her profile?"

"It's all set to private," I say with regret. The number of hours I've wasted at work attempting to find out more about her is shameful, but it didn't stop me trying. "I found out where her tattoo studio is, though. Do you think I should send her a present back?"

Ellen considers the question for a moment, then shakes her head. "No. She's clearly more experienced in this regard than you are. Let her take the lead and just do as she says. Isn't that what you're into—submission?"

"I guess so." Again, I feel myself blush. Maybe I over-shared a little, but I had to get it off my chest and if it gives Ellen ammunition to tease me at a later date, then so be it. The thought of tonight makes me wet and I shift in my chair in an attempt to release some of the building tension in my throbbing clit. My body has been on fire all morning.

Ellen suddenly perks up as if she's had a light bulb moment. "Hey, maybe that's why you had such a shit sex life with Brian. Because you're gay."

"Maybe," I mutter. "Or maybe our sex life sucked because Brian was a selfish prick."

"Could be. I always thought he was a bit standoffish, can't imagine him being very passionate in bed." Ellen's shrugs. "Anyway, this is not about Brian. Let's talk some more about your mystery lady. Her profile picture is visible, right? Let me see it."

I grin as I look up Syd's picture and show it to her. I've

opened it at least twenty times today and know it won't be the last.

"Fuck me, she's hot," Ellen says studying the picture. "Kind of androgynous, and very attractive. Hmm…" She bites her lip and cocks her head, zooming in. "Nice eyes too, fierce and icy. Have you thought of calling her? Aren't you curious about her voice? I bet she sounds sexy…"

"Of course I've thought about it. I've been imagining her voice a million times, but I don't think I'll call her. The idea terrifies me and besides, who knows how many women she's doing this with? There could be dozens."

"Or maybe she's just doing it with you."

"Yeah, right. People don't just single out one person and then go that far with them. It must be some kind of weird fetish." I shrug. "Not that I mind."

"But if she tells you to call her…" Ellen chuckles. "Then trust me, you will, honey. I have a feeling you'll do anything she asks you to."

6

_____

Our exchange tonight starts out with Syd sending me a picture with the caption: *'Figured I owe you this.'* A flutter runs through me when I open it and see Syd in nothing but a pair of white panties. She's on a bed, one arm bent, her hand resting under her head. Unable to take my eyes off her beautiful breasts, I stare at them for what feels like an eternity, then lower my gaze to her smooth thighs. Unconsciously, I ball my hands into fists, aching to touch her. The bird's-eye view tells me she's using a selfie stick again.

'You have a selfie stick,' I type, and finish with a laughing emoji. *'But I love the picture and yes, you did owe me one.'* Feeling brave, I add: *'Planning on taking any more off?'*

'Maybe. And yes, I am using a selfie stick. Joke all you want; it comes in surprisingly handy in situations like this.'

'So you've done this before, have you?' I ask, glad to have a way in without sounding clingy.

'Once or twice. But it's been a while.'

I'm not sure if I believe her but decide I don't really care. We're in different time zones and, although this is sexual and highly intense for me, at the same time it's neither physical nor emotional. *'I like your tattoos. Did you design them yourself?'* Apart from the various tattoos covering her arm, she has a prominent one on her left thigh too; a monochrome dragon that snakes around her leg.

'Yes I did. Glad you approve, I like my job. And I've been imagining you in the office... I love a woman in charge. It's sexy.'

'Not sure if it's sexy, but it pays the bills.' I smile as I send it, conscious of the luxury surrounding me. My ocean-view penthouse was not cheap, but I figured I deserved a reward for all my years of hard work, and it seemed fitting recompense for my soulless marriage to a man who'd grown to be very wealthy by the time we separated. I moved in here shortly after my divorce and have loved every minute of living by the sea. The scent of the ocean from my bedroom balcony in the morning is priceless, and the view during sunset still takes my breath away.

'Trust me, it is.'

'I think being a tattoo artist is pretty sexy too,' I reply, smug that I'm finally able to engage in flirty dialogue without my nerves getting in the way.

'Maybe I'll ink you one day.'

The usual wink emoji that follows, and her provocative statement, make me clench my teeth and squeeze my thighs together. But then this woman could talk about the weather and it would still turn me on. I've honestly never even considered getting a tattoo, but the idea of her marking me is arousing. *'That sounds interesting.'* I wait for her to reply and then wait some more. Am I boring her? Frustrated, I get up and pour myself a scotch. The message I come back to makes me take in a quick breath.

'Can I call you on here? Video call?'

Oh my God. She wants to call me. And not just a call, a video call. Worried about how I look, I rush over to the mirror and run a hand through my tangled hair, regretting not putting any makeup on after my shower. My hair is still wet and I feel a little silly for just having washed myself before a chat conversation because it's not like she'll be able to smell the lotion I applied, or the perfume I'm wearing, or feel the smoothness of my freshly shaved legs. I should have dried my hair and put on some makeup instead, but I look okay, I assure myself, even though the prospect of hearing her voice and seeing her makes me tremble in anticipation. I stopped smoking years ago and haven't felt the craving since, but I could really do with a cigarette right now.

'*Well?*' she asks.

Sitting back down, I look at my phone, my thumb hovering over it, hesitantly. This is moving a little fast for me, but I want it nevertheless. '*Okay.*'

It only takes seconds for my phone to ring and it feels surreal when I see her name on the screen, waiting for me to pick up. I slide a trembling finger across the screen and hold my breath as her face comes into focus.

"Hi," I say, suddenly sounding shy and hating myself for it. "This is weird."

"Hi, Val." Syd's clearly a lot more confident than I am, her low and slightly raspy voice loud and clear as she smiles into the camera. I love how she says my name and shortens it. No one ever does that. "Too weird?"

"No, it's fine, I just need a little time to get used to it. Not working tonight either?" I ask, in need of something to talk about. The question is irrelevant because we both know what we want. Useless small talk is one of my downfalls. It's one of the few things that tells people I'm anxious, but being calm and collected most of the time, it doesn't happen very often. That, and pulling at my eyelashes, which I realize I'm currently doing—the sudden jolt of pain as I twist two dark hairs between my thumb and index-finger bringing me back to the present.

"I'm not open today; I have other things I need to work on."

"Oh. Like what?"

"I'll tell you about it some time." Her smile widens and it's so sexy that it's hard to look at her without squirming. "Let's face it, we're not here to talk about me. We're here because I'm going to make you come again... hard." It's clear she likes my reaction to her words because her eyes darken at my parting lips and hitching breath. "I love your voice, by the way," she continues as if we're having a perfectly normal conversation. "It's so sweet and feminine."

I still don't know what to say so I wait for her to continue. The woman turns me on like nothing else, and the way she looks at me makes me melt. Now that we're actually talking, the impact of her words multiplies by a million, because I can hear in her voice how much she wants this and can see the desire in her gaze. She's holding her phone close to her face; her eyes are in sharp focus, and her glistening bottom lip looks wonderfully inviting. I've never felt an urge to kiss anyone so strong.

"Do you want to show me what you're wearing under that robe?" The way she says it makes it sound more like a demand than a question, and I find myself instantly untying it and opening it for her before directing my phone toward my breasts.

"Nothing," I answer as my hand runs over my breasts, parting the fabric.

"Nothing..." She licks her lips. "I like that. Show me the rest."

I point my phone down, over my belly, then move down

farther, exposing my pussy, my thighs and my legs, stretched out in front of me, one crossed over the other.

"Perfect." She pauses and says: "Spread them."

"What?" I must sound utterly shocked because she chuckles in amusement.

"Spread your legs for me. I want to see all of you."

Swallowing hard, I make sure to keep the phone away from my face, hiding my red-hot cheeks. I'm terrified but also intensely turned on and I don't even need to check to know how wet I am. Slowly I spread my legs and point the phone's camera lens above my swollen lips.

"Mmm..." Syd moans, and it makes me moan quietly too. "Is there a coffee table by the couch?"

"Yes." I frown and point the camera back to my face. "Why?"

"Stand your phone on there and make sure I can see all of you. You're going to need both hands for this."

I scan the room in search of something to lean my phone against, her instruction proving difficult as the apartment is pretty much clutter-free. Eventually my eye finds the perfect prop. My heavy crystal scotch glass will work and I move it back, then place my phone at an angle so that most of me is visible. Syd does the same, putting her phone on something next to her bed. She turns her head to face me, biting her lip.

"See? This works."

"It does." A smile plays around my lips as I enjoy the side view of her body and she seems more than pleased with seeing mine. "Now what?" I ask, dying to touch myself. The pulsating throb in my clit makes me shift and move my legs restlessly. I'm highly aroused and in need of release. When she lowers her panties and kicks them off, I can't keep my gaze away from her. The thin strip of dark hair doesn't cover much of her modesty and the need to taste her is so overwhelming that I'm seriously doubting my sexuality now. I never longed for a man the way I long for her.

"Do you have my present there?"

"Yes," I say, grabbing the pink toy from the floor next to me.

"I want to watch you while you use it. Touch your breasts. Pinch your nipples for me. Imagine they're my hands on you." Her sultry voice cuts through me, luring me into doing whatever it is she wants. "Yes, like that," she continues when my nails scrape over my breasts, leaving red marks. "Now turn on the vibrator."

I moan softly as I touch myself and lock my eyes with hers in the camera. At the same time, I can see myself lying on the couch in the second screen above. My legs spread, my breasts heaving up and down, my face an expression of pure lust. Pinching my nipples so hard that my hips buck, and my chest shoots up, I lower the vibrator between my legs. It feels incredible, and her smile tells me she likes what she sees. My back arches at the contact and I lose myself in mind-blowing insanity as the thrilling sensation against my clit grows, making my pussy tingle. As she watches me come undone, Syd's hand reaches between her own legs and the sight of it makes me gasp. The way her face pulls into an expression of delight, all the time keeping her eyes on me, causes my juices to drip out of me. I see her fingers dip inside her and begin to feel dizzy.

"Push it down harder," she says in a breathy voice, then moans louder as she starts fucking herself with her fingers.

I love watching her so much that I can barely concentrate on what I'm doing, yet my body is screaming out for more. When I increase the pressure of the vibrator, it hits me so hard that I levitate off the couch, my hips moving frantically as I'm unable to stop my climax from taking over. Seeing that she's close too, from the way her body is moving in sync with mine, I let go, and only seconds later, she explodes too. She's loud and I don't hold back either. The sound of our combined cries is the most erotic thing I've ever heard, so powerful that I know I'll remember this moment forever. It's strange how we keep our eyes locked as it's somehow more intimate than it should be in our situation but I'm unable to look away. Seeing her eyelids flutter in ecstasy is beautiful and I feel privileged to witness her moment. A little later, she starts to laugh, and I laugh too because I know we're both thinking how ridiculously good this is.

"Are you okay?" I ask, because she suddenly looks terribly serious when she lets out a deep sigh and turns on her side to face me fully. The way we're lying, and the way our cameras are positioned, makes me feel like I'm there with her.

"Yeah." She nods and smiles. "I just didn't expect something like this to be so good, that's all. You drive me wild."

"Same," I say. "You're incredible. It's amazing to watch you and it makes me want to touch you." The words are out before I've had the time to think them through.

"I want to touch you too." Syd sits up and pulls the bedsheets over her naked body. "In fact, there's not much I wouldn't give to have my hands on you right now, but we're not exactly walking distance, so let's agree to meet on here again tomorrow, shall we? A little later though, because I'm working."

"That's good for me. I'll be here." I want to keep talking to her, simply lying here like this together, but I don't know where to start or how to express my thoughts. From the way she keeps leaving, I'm guessing she doesn't want this to get too personal and I can understand that. What would be the point? It's not like any more will come of this. Still, I want to know more about her, but just as I open my mouth, she gets up and gives me a wink.

"I have to go now. Another present will be arriving for you tomorrow."

"Okay..." I chuckle, hiding my disappointment of having to hang up already, wishing I could fast-forward time. "I can't wait to see it."

7

The day is creeping by while I'm waiting for an email from the mail room to let me know my package has arrived. My schedule is clear today as I need to catch up on admin and prepare a presentation for the rest of the board tomorrow. It's still staggeringly hard to concentrate but I manage somehow, and I'm almost done with the seventh slide when my assistant knocks on the door.

"Hi, Nyssa," I say, trying to keep the irritation out of my voice as I clearly told her not to interrupt.

"I'm sorry to disturb you, Valerie, but I just happened to be downstairs to pick up the mail and I heard a delivery lady say your name, so I thought I'd bring it up for you."

My eyes widen as I stare at the black box she's holding, and my first thought is that I hope she didn't see the delivery truck. Somehow, I manage to compose myself and wave in the direction of the coffee table next to the sofa. "Thank you. Just put it over there." After that, I ignore her and turn back to my screen, pretending to be focused because I can't look her in the eyes right now. Does she know? Did the delivery lady have a logo on her shirt or whatever she was wearing? Was she wearing much at all? I looked up the store yesterday and their branding is very clear. *Naughty Delights.* Going on the name, there would be no mistake about what they sell.

As soon as Nyssa closes the door behind her, I get up and walk over to the hallway-facing window. I'm about to close the blinds when I change my mind. If Nyssa sees me closing them, she'll be sure to think the package is suspicious and she's not shy of gossip; I've overheard her talking in the canteen. Although I can barely contain my curiosity, I leave the box on the table and decide to wait until I'm home.

Three hours later, I'm finally in my kitchen with the black box on the counter. Although these presents might be just as much for her own pleasure, I don't remember the last time someone got me a gift other than flowers or a bottle of scotch, and it makes me giddy. I kick off my heels and close my eyes at the feeling of cold tiles under my sore feet, then take off my black blazer and my pants, leaving me only in my top and panties. Taking my clothes and shoes off is my favorite part of the day and when I'm at home, I never wear much other than my robe. Lying on the couch near-naked with microwave or takeout meals might seem sad to some, but for me it's bliss after a hectic day at work.

Sure, I go out. Sometimes because I have to and sometimes because I want to. But mostly, I'm very happy being home by myself reading. The fact that the lesbian erotica I was so hooked on has now turned into reality, is something I wouldn't have dared hope for, only a week ago.

A flutter of excitement tugs at me as I pull at the pink

ribbon and open the lid. It's another vibrator, but a larger, phallic shaped one this time. The design is pink and stream-lined, just like the previous toy but clearly designed for different use. Immediately, I feel immense desire well up, my mind going places I'm not quite ready for yet. Pulling at my turtleneck top, I feel hot and flushed, and an urgent need to take everything off chases me out of the kitchen. I make my way through the long hallway, then into the master bedroom where my housekeeper has done an excellent job of making the bed look immaculate and turn on the rain shower on the other side of the frosted glass wall behind my bed.

Removing the rest of my clothes, I take the time to observe myself in the mirror. I don't look bad for forty-one, even though I never bother with the gym or diets. Maybe I'm too busy to be excessively unhealthy, or maybe I'm just lucky to have my father's genes. Running a hand through my dark hair, I find myself feeling sensual tonight. It's not some-thing I ever felt while I was with my ex-husband and even before that, I don't think I've thought of myself as a very sexual being. Ironically, sex is all I can think of now, and as I step under the shower, I know it's because of Syd, who has awoken this fire in me. It started as a small, curious glow that spontaneously combusted the moment we got personal and the flames are now rising to unpredictable heights. If I fuel this incendiary thing between us even more, I'm afraid of what will happen.

8

"Hi." Syd seems genuinely excited when I pick up.

"Hi," I reply with a grin plastered all over my face. I don't usually show my emotions so easily, but I'm unable to hide my happiness at seeing her again. "Thank you for the present. I feel like I should send you something back."

"No need." Syd gives me a wink. "I like this arrangement and as long as you do too, we're fine."

"I like it very much." There's no point claiming otherwise because I know my face speaks for itself. I want this so badly. No... I need this. Syd is all I'm able to think of and by now, she's become some unhealthy obsession, like I've only ever seen in movies. My attempts to find out more about her have failed, with only her Instagram account being public, and unfortunately it doesn't show much other than her work.

"So, did you open it?" She's lying on her bed again, this time dressed in a denim shirt and a pair of white Calvin Klein boy shorts. Her hair is slicked back after a recent shower and she looks like a model. I remind myself to keep my mouth closed as I take her in.

"I did." I hesitate. "I've never used one like this before."

"That's okay. I'm honored to witness your first time." Syd licks her lips and lowers her phone so only her face is visible now. "I've been thinking about you a lot today. You're very distracting, Val."

"Same here," I reply. "Especially when you send me presents like this one." I hold up the vibrator and open my robe a little further so she can see my breasts. Any lingering reservation has gone out of the window, any doubts I had last week have vanished like they were never there. I feel free with her and I truly believe there are very few things I wouldn't do if she asked me. "I've been thinking of you too."

"Good." Her lips pull into a smirk as she stares at my breasts and shifts on the mattress. "Will you do something for me?"

"Depends," I reply, a teasing tone ringing through my words.

Syd looks into my eyes and smiles. Her dimples turn me into a pool of liquid desire, and I nod. "I want you to turn around and sit up. Place the phone on the seat of the couch you so I can see you from below. Then open your robe. I want to know what it would look like if you were straddling me."

I frown, working out the logistics in my head, then do as she says. As I sit down on my knees and look at the screen, I can see myself from below; a part of my stomach, the swell of my breasts with taut nipples sticking out and my face, looking down at her.

"God, you're so fucking sexy," she says, looking up at me through the screen in return. "I love this angle." She's unbuttoning her shirt, teasingly slow. It really does look like

I'm sitting on top of her, and I feel an explosive need to reach through my phone and rip open her shirt. Finally, her breasts are exposed as she opens it and takes it off. She's not wearing a bra, and the sight of her nipples makes me salivate, as I imagine sucking them hard into my mouth.

Apparently, this is not just a fantasy anymore, because I feel an overwhelming physical urge to be with a woman. Not just any woman, but with her, and it's so strong that I might lose my mind if I don't get to touch her. She's so close, yet so far away and I'm afraid it's not enough anymore.

"I want you," I whisper, and I can hardly believe that I'm saying this to her, but I am. She's all I want right now, maybe ever.

"I want you too," Syd says, and I know she means it. She looks tortured, the way she stares at my breasts without being able to touch them, and I feel the same. "Imagine being on top of me," she continues, locking her eyes with mine. "Imagine I'm wearing a strap-on. I want you to use the toy, ride it like you would ride me." She pauses. "I want to be deep inside you, Val."

Her words have me writhing, gasping for air. My hands shake as I get up on my knees, adjusting the phone so she can see all of me, and place the device between my legs. I don't need lube; I'm incredibly wet already and the thought of sliding it inside me while she watches makes my juices flow even more. "Like this?" I ask, inching down on the vibrator, the tip of it pressing between my sensitive lips.

"Perfect." Syd looks totally turned on as she slides her hand inside her boy shorts and watches me. "Now lower yourself into it." Her eyes meet mine and for a moment, it's like she's in the room with me. "Feel me sliding inside you."

It feels impossibly tight as I sit down on the phallic shaped silicone, and I moan as little by little each delicious inch stretches me open. It's the most private thing I've ever done with anyone. My eyes flutter closed as I envelop the toy, moaning louder now.

"How does it feel?" she asks.

"Good," I whisper. "It feels really good."

Syd looks pleased with my answer, her own breath quickening. "There's a button at the base. Press it."

I reach between my legs and feel the slight bump on the sleek surface. When I press it, a groan escapes my mouth and my eyes widen. The vibrating sensations feel amazing inside me.

"Ride it," she commands, and I do as she says.

My back arches each time I lower myself, my hips rolling and my shoulders and head falling back as I take on a slow and steady rhythm. I'm entranced, delirious, and I try to stay focused on her face and her voice, moaning each time the shaft enters me. She loves watching me; I know it, and it only turns me on more. "I'm going to come," I say through hitched breaths, feeling so entranced by what we're doing that I can barely speak.

"Yes..." Syd groans and her hand moves faster, making herself come too as I give in to my climax, clenching around the shaft. I imagine her strap-on being there, or her fingers, feeling my need for her. I'm vaguely aware of my body shaking, the noises I make, my facial expressions raw and wild, but in this moment, I don't care what I look like. It's earth-shatteringly good, and I regret it when we both come down and stare at each other in disbelief, because I don't want this to be over just yet.

9

"God..." She mutters, looking at me through hazy eyes, and I still feel like I'm sitting on top of her.

I see my image on the half screen, the curve of my breasts visible from underneath, my hungry eyes looking down at her. "I know." I'm breathless as I wipe the sweat off my forehead. "That was amazing. Imagine..." I hate myself for saying it out loud again, but the words just roll off my tongue. It's not like I want to meet up. Or do I?

"Yeah," she says, as if reading my thoughts. "Imagine if we did this in real life. Sweating bodies, kissing, skin on skin, heavy breathing, the smell of sex in the room... It would be pretty damn good."

Laughing, I shake my head. "I don't know, I might not survive. This is almost too much already."

"There's no such thing as too much." Syd's expression turns serious again, and something tells me that maybe this isn't just a game to her. "Are you sure you're not in a relationship?"

"No," I say. "I'm divorced. Are you really single?"

"Yes." She hesitates. "So there's nothing stopping us from meeting up..."

My heart starts pounding in my chest because, although I've had that daydream many times since meeting Syd online, I've never actually entertained the idea of it becoming a reality. But then again, I never imagined us to be doing this either. "Do you really want to meet up?" I swallow hard and turn to lie down on my back, looking up at her. We're both in close-up now, and although it's crazy, it feels even more intimate than minutes ago when she watched me come while riding the vibrator. It's the vulnerability in her eyes, which I'm sure, is reflected in mine too. We're both scared because this is really, really good and God knows what will happen when we're face to face.

"You could come here," Syd suggests after a long pause. "Join me in my bed." She pats the empty space next to her. "Or I can come to you or we can meet up somewhere in the middle... It doesn't have to mean anything, I just want to fuck you, Val."

Her proposal terrifies me, yet I can hardly contain my excitement. "We could do that." I think it over for a beat, deciding that having her in my space is way too personal for me at this point. "I suppose I could come to you... I've actually never been to Canada." I'm half expecting her to back out, but she doesn't.

"That sounds good to me." She gives me a sexy smile. "I promise you won't regret it. I'm going to make your fuse blow like you can't even imagine."

Her confidence astounds me, and I'm trembling heavily, shaken by the idea of meeting up, but also so consumed by the thought of finally touching her. Is she really serious? "I have no doubt. I'm..." My voice trails away when a thought hits me. What if I'm crap in bed? I want this, but I won't even know what I'm doing. "There's something I haven't told you," I confess.

"Okay..." Syd frowns. "Tell me."

I take a deep breath and decide to just blurt it out. "I've never been with a woman before." She needs to know this, or she'll be disappointed when we meet. If it makes her back out, then so be it.

"What?" Syd looks lost as she studies me. "How?" There's a silence between us. "But you're... you're really into this."

"I am. But I only discovered the books last year and joined the book club after my divorce. To a man," I add. "The first lesbian erotica book I read... well, I ordered it by accident, and then I couldn't stop reading them. That's why I joined the book club, to get recommendations." I'm convinced she's going to change her mind but instead she shakes her head as if she can't quite believe what I'm telling her.

"So you were married to a man?"

"Yes."

"And you're straight?"

"Kind of..." I shrug. "I'm not sure."

Syd stares at me for another moment and I'd kill to know what she's thinking. "That's okay," she finally says. "I'll be honest with you; it was the last thing I expected after what we've been doing, but I'm kind of excited about the idea of being your first." She brushes a lock of dark hair away from her forehead and shoots me a flirty look. "So don't worry, I'll teach you everything I know. And I know a lot."

A blush hits my cheeks and I'm conscious of the fact that

my insecurities are showing. No one has seen me like this, letting my guard down, not even my ex-husband. "Meeting up... it's kind of bold, don't you think?" I ask. "I mean, we've only known each other—and when I say 'known' I mean that in the broadest sense of the word—for ten days. I don't think anyone would even consider getting on a flight for someone after ten days. Isn't it very..."

"Very soon?" Syd finishes my sentence. "Yes, it's very soon. Stupid soon." She smiles, her dimples turning me into putty in an instant. "But then again, it's just sex. We're meeting up to have sex, not to get married." A faint sigh passes her lips, as if she too knows that it makes no sense at all, even if it's just sex. "How about we wait a couple of weeks? We both have lives and need to make arrangements so if by that time we still feel like we want to meet as much as we do now, we'll figure out where and when."

"Okay," I say with a mixture of relief and disappointment. If it was up to me, I'd be there tomorrow, but right now I'm not thinking clearly, and if I'm being honest with myself, I don't think I'm ready yet either.

"And if you change your mind, that's fine of course," Syd adds. "There's no pressure and you can tell me to leave you alone anytime."

At that, I laugh because the chances of me growing tired of her are about as slim as me getting back with Brian. I want her with every fibre of my being, every cell in my body. Just the thought of her makes me weak, taking away any sense of logic that I normally hold onto so dearly. "I doubt that's going to happen," I say, shooting her a flirty look. "But the same counts for you. If you get bored of calling me, just let me know and I won't bug you anymore."

Syd's eyes narrow as her face pulls into an amused grin,

and she tilts her head in the most adorable way. "I doubt that will happen either. So for now, let's keep meeting up online after work when we're both available." She quirks an eyebrow. "It's too good not to, right?"

10

"I'm going to see her," I tell Ellen over cocktails. We're in a private members' club in Hollywood, the female equivalent of a traditional gentlemen's club, I suppose. No men are allowed here, and it's nice to go somewhere with exquisite service without having to dodge guys trying to impress you by sending over drinks and starting unwanted conversations. We only ever go here when we're planning to have a serious talk, or gossip over their indulgent drinks' menu. Any night spent in *Tigress* is a guarantee for a headache the next morning, but I don't care because I really need to blow off steam to someone.

"You're fucking with me." Ellen looks at me as if I've lost my mind, and right then, I'm wondering if maybe I have. Am I really sure I want to do this? Saying it out loud suddenly sounds daunting. I must be insane to get on a plane for someone I only met online three weeks ago, and a woman no less. The money is no issue, and it's not like I've taken any vacations in the past couple of years, but it does seem like a mad idea. I don't know Syd, and I don't even know if I'll feel the same when we meet face to face, yet the prospect of making love with her in person has me consumed day and night.

"No, I'm serious," I say, taking a sip of my old fashioned as I sink deeper into the red, velvet couch. The club is situated on the roof of a tall building, a breathtaking view over the City of Angels stretching before us. Just like Ellen, I appreciate the finer things in life and Syd is no doubt one of them.

"You're going to fly to Canada and then what? Have endless wild sex?"

"Yes." I shrug. "I have no choice. If I don't do it, I'll always wonder what it could have been like. I crave her and the craving's only growing."

"Jesus." Ellen chuckles. "What has she done to you?" she asks.

"I'm not sure." It's weird not to be sure, as I'm always so self-assured. "All I know is that I was straight and dominant —at least in my job if my colleagues' comments are anything to go by—and admittedly, perhaps a little dull in my private life. But apparently that's not who I am anymore. Or maybe I never was that person." The thought of having lived a lie for most of my life makes me feel a little sick. "What if I am gay?" I ask. "I've never felt so sexually fulfilled as I do now. What a fucking waste of time. All those years with men..."

"Nothing's a waste," Ellen says, putting on her 'I know it all' tone. "None of my husbands were a waste of time. They gave me nice houses, cool cars, an amazing collection of designer handbags and club memberships for life." She spreads her arms and gestures to the opulent room we are now sitting in. Crystal chandeliers twinkle from the ceiling and an immensely talented pianist sits behind a shiny black grand piano, whilst beautiful waitresses in little red dresses flutter around the room like butterflies, topping up Champagne and serving the latest finger foods. "And your life wasn't a waste either. That prick got you where you are today, and the divorce only added to your capital."

"Hey, that's not true," I object. "My career has nothing to do with Brian, I did that all by myself. So yes, it was a waste," I mumble, downing the rest of my cocktail. I don't buy Ellen's excuse. She was never happy when she was married, and neither was I. Frankly, I don't see how having more money makes that any better. But then again, I like to work, and Ellen doesn't. I like the power it gives me, the respect. I get excited by accomplishment; Ellen gets excited by Veuve Clicquot and Prada. "But we'll see. I might not feel the same when I get there, anything is possible."

"I think you're going to enjoy yourself more than you can imagine," Ellen says, holding her glass up in a toast. "How long are you going for?"

"Two nights."

"Smart move." Ellen nods in agreement. "One night is too short, but if it's not for you, or if she turns out to be a lunatic, you can always spend a night at the airport or change your flight." She waves at the waitress and points at our glasses, letting her know we'd like another. "So what about *her*, then?"

"What about her?" I ask, not understanding where Ellen is going as she inclines her head toward the waitress.

"Would you sleep with *her*?"

My eyes follow the blonde woman, whose hips sway as she makes her way to the bar. She's pretty, sure, and her body is amazing, but there's something missing. I shake my head. "No, not feeling it."

"What about her, then?" Ellen then nods toward one of the customers, a redhead in a booth behind us. Again, she's attractive, but I can't imagine myself naked with her. Not like with Syd, who's been on my mind twenty-four-seven.

"No. I'm not attracted to anyone apart from Syd," I admit. "I don't think sex is the same if the energy isn't there, man or woman."

Ellen shrugs. "I have no problem with that part but hey, each to their own." She grins, and I suspect she's had many an interesting night with her never-ending plethora of toy boys. "Anyway," she continues, "we need to go shopping."

I smile at that because I've been thinking exactly the same. "Yes. I need new lingerie."

"And you need some snazzy outfits. You can't go there looking like you're heading for a board meeting."

"What's wrong with my suits?" I regard my perfectly cut black suit that fits me like a glove. It's my armor, my protection, and in essence, it's who I am. Smart and no-nonsense.

"There's nothing wrong with them..." Ellen purses her lips as she regards me. "But you might want to get something that comes off easily. No one wants to attempt removing a turtle neck and having to peel off three layers of clothing when they're desperate to fuck you. You need something that she can simply hike up. However, the heels might come in handy." She snickers behind her hand as she utters the last sentence.

I laugh it off, but the thought turns me on. Ellen is right; I can't rock up in a pantsuit, it's far too complicated. "Okay, let's go shopping." I take my second cocktail from the waitress, again appreciating her looks. I might not want to sleep with her, but I do think she's way more attractive than any man I've ever dated, so maybe that says something about me after all.

"Perfect." Ellen takes a slug of her drink and slams it down. "I'm going to turn you into a smokin' hot sex kitten."

11

---

s this me? Ellen assured me it was, but I know she's lying. She's never seen me in a dress before and frankly, neither have I. The feeling of my bare legs under the delicate fabric is nice though, and I turn around in front of the mirror once more, inspecting myself from the back in the lavish fitting room. I feel sexy as I take myself in; my curves and legs on display like I'm offering myself up. Isn't that what I'm doing? Grooming myself, preparing for the moment I'll present myself to her? Wondering how a woman can make me feel feminine while no man ever could, I hike up the hem just a little, imagining her hands on my thighs.

"You okay in there?" Ellen yells. Too distracted by my wild fantasies, I fail to answer, and she lets herself in. "Oh my God, Valerie! You look exquisite!" Her eyes roam over me; from the low cleavage of the black silk dress to my bare legs and my ankles in the black high heeled shoes she chose for me. "I think I might be questioning my own sexuality now," she jokes, pinching my behind. "Especially if you're going to wear that other stuff underneath."

I slap her hand away and laugh as I glance down at the bag with lingerie I've already purchased. "Cut it out, Ellen. I know for a fact you're super straight. You haven't stopped talking about that yoga teacher since we got here."

Ellen sighs and pulls a dramatic face. "Yes, Sadiq has been a blessing. He's so strong and passionate and..." She snaps out of her indecent thoughts and turns her attention back to me. "But then so are you, honey. You're a blessing to anyone who gets permission to touch that cute ass of yours. Syd is going to be one lucky woman."

I shiver at the sound of Syd's name and suddenly feel insecure. Next week, I'm flying out to Canada explicitly with the plan of having sex with a stranger, yet I have no idea what I'm doing because she'll be my first woman. We've spoken to each other almost every day, and even more so in the past week, messaging back and forth whenever we've had the chance. There's no doubt that I'm on her mind too; she's always quick to reply and never fails to let me know how much she wants me. Still, I can't shake off the thought that I might not be who she thinks I am.

Normally, I don't care what people think of me. Being in a position where department budgets depend on me hasn't necessarily made me popular, but it's made me grow a thick skin, and I have no desire to be 'popular' with my employees. I'm just doing my job, whether they like it or not. Honestly, I've never cared if people like me in my personal life either. Although there's a small group of women I meet up with regularly, Ellen is the only person I actually love to spend time with. She's just easy going, always her same funny self, and if anything good has come from my failed marriage to Brian, it's her.

"Here, try this one on too." She holds up a red, bias-cut satin dress and mischievously bats her eyelashes.

"Don't push it." I shake my head and laugh. "I still want to feel like myself. That one's way too revealing." Taking a deep breath, I nod at my reflection. "I'll take this one. And the shoes."

"Ever been to Quebec?" I ask Ellen when we're guided to a table in the department store's restaurant. I've asked for a table outside on the roof, as I really need some fresh air after finally finding the dress I'll be wearing when I first meet Syd. A tremor rocks my body when I imagine the moment, and it's suddenly starting to feel very real.

"Of course not." Ellen snorts and slumps down in her chair. "Why in the flying fuck would I want to go there?"

"Why not? I've heard it's nice." I sit down opposite her and stretch my tired legs out before me. My suits work well for the office, but up here it's a little warm, so I take off my blazer and hang it over the back of my chair.

"I've heard the suburbs are nice too, doesn't mean I want to go there." Ellen scans the menus the waiter hands her and smirks. "I doubt they have 1966 Dom Pérignon on the wine lists in Quebec."

"You're such a snob. It's Canada, not Kazakhstan." I chuckle and look up at the waiter. "I'll have a black coffee and a bottle of Perrier, please."

"No, she won't." Ellen waves a hand, stopping him from typing it into his handheld device. "We'll have a bottle of Dom to share. And a dozen oysters, Tabasco on the side. This lady is going to Canada," she adds in a stage whisper. "So she'll be indulging while she still can."

"You're the worst," I say as the waiter shoots her a puzzled look, nods and walks off. "I need my caffeine fix. Normally I'd be on my third by now."

Ellen shakes her head. "Don't argue with me, we need to celebrate your new outfit and the fact that you're going to be having sex soon. Real sex, not the phone kind. Do you even remember what it's like to feel a hot, sweaty body against your own? And Syd's will be a woman's body no less..."

"Hush, Ellen! Keep your voice down for God's sake." I look around, nervously scanning the place for familiar faces. Thankfully, there's no one here I know, just the usual downtown LA crowd; businesspeople, young moms with hideously expensive strollers and women like myself and Ellen, resting after spending too much money. Through the murmur of voices, I pick up on things like: 'My husband found our nanny on an escort site so we had to let her go', and: 'Can I really still get away with white jeans at thirty?' It's all terribly shallow but I guess Ellen's statement about Canada is just as bad, so I don't share their ramblings. A woman sends her food back, claiming it doesn't look 'pretty' enough, and two men next to us are nibbling on the forty-two-dollar banana bread, served on hand-painted slate. As soon as it hits me that bananas have become the latest luxury food item, I decide Quebec will be a refreshing break.

12

My legs feel like jelly as the sliding doors open up into the arrivals area before me. Although I flew business, giving me the opportunity to freshen up on the flight, I'm clammy again already and for a moment, I consider running off and hiding somewhere. What if she doesn't like me in real life? What if I'm not the woman she thought I was? What if she isn't the woman I thought she was? What if we have nothing to talk about? The answers become clear soon enough, as all the what ifs evaporate when I catch a glimpse of her standing behind the barrier, waiting for me.

She's taller than I expected her to be, but other than that, she looks exactly the same. Tight, low jeans hug her hips and she's wearing a blue checked shirt under a thin, olive-green jacket. It's strange seeing her in clothes, rather than in just a shirt and her underwear, and the casual air she gives off sets me on fire. This is her, the real her, and she's even sexier in real life than I imagined. Her face lights up when she catches sight of me, and I rush over to meet her.

"Hey," she says, her tone a lot more confident than I feel right now. Her remarkable icy blue eyes pierce through me, making me shiver. There's no doubt that we have chemistry; I'm drawn to her like a magnet and my heart is beating out of my chest. Just her nearness makes me aroused and wet, and I can see from the way she's taking me in that she wants to devour me too.

"Look at you..." She gives me a flirty smile, her gaze raking over me. "Are you trying to kill me in that dress?" Then her eyes drop to my mouth and she inches closer. I feel her breath on my lips and the heat from her body as we linger on the spot, breathing in each other's air for what feels like an eternity. The pull between us is immense and I want nothing more than her mouth on mine.

"Not here," she whispers. "I want you alone when I kiss you for the first time." I nod, and my breath hitches when she moves closer. "You have no idea what you're doing to me, Val."

If she feels anything like I do, I have a pretty good idea, but I'm so overwhelmed that I have trouble forming a sentence. "Take me somewhere," I finally reply, then follow her out of the airport.

The parking lot is dark and quiet, and her Jeep is parked in a far corner. I cross my arms and shiver as she puts my suitcase in the trunk and slams it closed. Despite it being summer it's a little chilly for the black slip dress and high heels I bought with Ellen, but my lined Burberry trench coat keeps at least part of me warm.

"Are you cold?" she asks, taking a step toward me, wedging me between the car and her body.

"A little." I'm aware of how my chest is heaving, my lips parting in hunger each time she looks at me.

"We'll have to do something about that, then." A smile plays around her lips as she cups my face in her hands and tilts her head, leaning into me. For a moment, she hesitates as if giving me time to change my mind, but I want her so badly that I run my fingers through her hair and pull her in. Our mouths clash together in a passionate dance, lust building inside of me, almost choking me with unfettered desire. Her lips are soft, her tongue like silk as she deepens the kiss with an urgency I've never known. I feel like she's swallowing me whole, making me disappear into her embrace. Our kiss is all consuming and our moans echo off the parking lot walls while our hands roam freely, tugging at each other's hair.

Kissing a woman, kissing her, is mind-blowing, so different to what I imagined. My body reacts with a feverish need as she presses herself tighter against me. She's soft and she smells incredible but it's not her perfume that enthralls me. It's her very own scent, the scent of her skin that rings through the subtle sweetness of her shampoo. It's astonishing how much you miss when you're not face to face. Although I feel like I know her, and am technically familiar with her body, I realize that there is so much more that makes her who she is. The way her hands feel as they slide down to my waist; pinching me as if she too has only now become aware of how amazing our chemistry is. Her taste, her tongue, her lips, her hands, her breath, everything... It's electric; the buzz of the contact making us both insatiable as we moan then break apart, knowing we won't be able to stop if we continue any longer.

"Fuck," I whisper, subconsciously running my fingertips along my lips. It's not just the feel of her and her smell; it's the air she has about her, the glow that radiates off her. I can see now that she is someone people like to be around, someone who draws attention with her mysterious and intriguing aura. She oozes sexuality. "That was..." I stop myself as I have no words for how that kiss felt, and all I can think of is that I want more.

"Not freaked out?" She asks with a sultry look in her eyes, already knowing the answer.

"No, quite the opposite."

"You look and smell amazing by the way," she whispers in my ear, leaning in against me again. We're clearly on the same wavelength.

"You too," I say, inhaling against her skin. It's like we're engaged in a dance of the senses, drinking each other in— our bodies coming to life at the stimulus of each other's touch. "Do you live far from here?"

"No, I live in the city. It's a short drive." She steps away, walks around the Jeep and opens the door for me. "I think you'll like it."

Already, I miss her body against mine and as I get into the car, my legs begin to quiver, knowing we'll be alone soon.

13

Syd's apartment, on the top floor of a charming old redbrick building, is small but has a lot of character with original beams, a fireplace, a low ceiling that gives a cozy feel to the place and a cast-iron balcony off the living room that's covered in ivy. It's located in one of the cutest pedestrian streets I've ever seen, at the foot of the cliff below Château Frontenac. I walk around and take it all in, smiling at the personal touches.

When you know very little about someone's day to-day life, you form an idea of them in your head, imagining their lives and surroundings. Nothing could have been further from how I pictured Syd's style, but at the same time it makes sense. It feels incredibly personal to be in her space, seeing her pictures on the walls and her things strewn around. It's not pristine like my penthouse, which is sterile and kept tidy by my housekeeper at all times, but it's got character and a very cool vibe to it.

"I love your apartment," I say, standing in front of the French doors that lead to the balcony which affords a view of the locals and tourists in the street below. She comes up behind me and slides my coat off my shoulders, so slowly that a hiss escapes my mouth. Everything is a new experience with her, and even the simple action of taking off my outerwear feels highly sensual.

"I waited seven years for something to come on the market here," she says, pouring me a glass of red wine without asking me what I want. "But I don't want to talk property right now. Do you?"

She doesn't need to remind me why I'm here, because touching her naked body is all I can think of. She hands me the glass of wine and stands behind me again, breathing against my shoulder while she runs a hand through my hair. I know she can see the hairs at the back of my neck rise, and I shiver when she traces a finger down it.

"Are you nervous, Val?" her voice in my ear is low and sultry, her lips brushing my earlobe. She's clearly a master of building anticipation, as I'd expected her to ravish me by now, but instead, she refrains from touching me much at all. It's like she's studying her prey before going in for the kill and it thrills me.

"Yes," I answer honestly. The way my heart is beating and my pulse is racing, there's no point of denying it; I know she can feel my anxiety coming off me in waves. I've never been this nervous in my life, but I've also never wanted anything so badly. Knowing she likes to be in charge, I stay where I am, facing the street.

Her hand curls around my waist and I hear her taking a sip of her wine. The touch feels electric and my abdomen tenses as she gropes me and pulls me firmly against her. I take in a quick breath, then hold it. She makes no point of putting me at ease, and I wonder if she likes that I'm scared. The public parking lot felt safe to me, but now that I'm in her lair, I tremble at the unknown. Still, there's no way I'd leave. Not now, because I'm so aroused that my panties are dripping wet.

I take a sip of my wine too, in an attempt to calm myself. I'm so not in control right now, yet our game makes me feel alive in a way I never imagined.

"Don't be nervous, there's no need," she finally mutters, deciding I've been tortured enough. Her mouth moves back to my ear again and she drags her tongue over it, then lingers there. Her ragged breath shoots through my body like a lightning bolt, making my pussy twitch. "I'm going to fuck you until you scream and after that, I'm going to teach you how to pleasure me." I can feel her lips pull into a smile as she delivers her blunt statement. "Would you like that?"

By now, I've melted into a pool of liquid desire, and I nod, at least I think I do.

Syd takes the glass from me and puts it on the coffee table, along with her own, then brushes my hair to one side, baring my shoulder. She slides the spaghetti strap of my dress down, then kisses my skin, working her way inward, toward my neck.

I moan when I feel her wet lips on me and cry out when she bites my neck. It doesn't hurt, but it shocks me. No one has bitten me before, and I tense up as her hands wrap around me tight, then move up to my breasts. She cups them through the fabric of my dress and squeezes them, reminding me I'm hers tonight. It feels so good that I throw my head back against her shoulder, my eyes fluttering when her thumbs brush over my already erect nipples. Even through the dress and my bra, I know she can feel how hard they are, how turned on I am. I can hardly believe a woman is kissing my neck and fondling me, her sweet scent and the softness of her cheek against mine reminding me that this will be a night to remember forever.

Her fingers spread apart as she moves her hands down my body, her movements symmetrical, pushing down on my skin as they settle on my thighs and lift up the hem of my dress, just like I imagined her doing in the fitting room when I bought it. The room is dimly lit and outside, nightlife is already buzzing in the early evening. Although I don't expect anyone on the street to look up and see me, there are similar apartments opposite us, and the idea of doing this here by the window feels lewd and dangerous.

"I like what you're wearing for me," she says in a seductive tone, tracing the edge of my stockings. She watches me in our reflection as she plays with the elastic of my black suspenders, then releases the fasteners one by one. I flinch as I feel them snap up against my hips, the simple action sending a shot of adrenaline through me.

Part of me wants to turn around and kiss her, and part of me is loving the voyeuristic nature of our actions. It's exciting, frightening, thrilling and when I feel her hands on my bare hips, I arch my back and let out another moan, louder this time. How does she do this to me? Driving me crazy with something as simple as her touch? She explores my body, moving farther up toward my belly, only slipping the tip of a finger under the waistband of my suspender belt for a moment before continuing, sliding her hands under my bra.

"You like that?" she asks, feeling my reaction that is nothing short of carnal. I groan as I dig my nails into her thighs behind me and feel her muscles tense through her jeans. My breath hitches at her warm hands on my breasts, and I cry out when she pinches my nipples, softly at first, then harder.

"Oh God..." I hold my breath again as she moves one of her hands back down, holding me against her with the other, still caressing my sensitive breasts. Her fingers slip between my thighs and she cups my pussy, feeling my liquid desire through the delicate fabric of my panties. My knees buckle and I can hardly stand up straight, her touch sending a flash of heat through me. Then she pulls her hands away, leaving me wanting more. I'm about to turn around when she grabs my shoulders and holds me in place.

"Wait. Let's take this off first." Syd lifts up my dress and pulls it over my head. I shiver at being half-naked in front of the window, and as the night begins to fall, I can see my own reflection clearly now. "Beautiful," she whispers, staring at me as she rests her cheek against mine. She unhooks my suspender belt and it drops to the floor, leaving me in my stockings, a pair of black lace panties and a black balcony bra that envelops my full breasts. I know I look good in the lingerie I bought with today in mind and I can tell Syd appreciates it as she looks me over. She caresses my behind and moves back up to my breasts, teasing me until I can't stand it anymore.

"Show me your bedroom." My voice is alien to me and reflects everything I'm not; insecure, fragile and needy. Although I hate how I sound, it seems to have the opposite effect on Syd, whose eyes flare up as she takes my hand and leads me back into the hallway.

There are three doors, and she opens the first. Only when we're inside her bedroom that is also street-facing, do I register she's still wearing all her clothes. I scan the room, half expecting to see a shelf of sex-toys on display but there's nothing but an antique four poster bed with matching nightstands, an original built-in closet, a rocking chair upholstered with gray velvet and a vanity table with a huge bunch of white lilies on top.

Syd turns on a lamp, bathing the room in a soft glow and

highlighting the delicate palette of whites and grays in which the walls and furniture are painted. She takes off her shirt and throws it over the chair in the corner. Left in her sports bra and jeans, she turns to me, giving me time to take her in. I need a moment to get used to seeing her in real life and although I'm almost paralyzed by my fear of the unknown, I want to touch her so badly that I manage to overcome my anxiety.

The tattoos on her arm I recognize, but the way her skin feels under my fingers when I trail a hand up to her shoulder is entirely new and I can tell it affects her as the hairs on her arms rise. She's soft, so soft. I explore her back, her abdomen, indulging in her toned and feminine body. My fingers tremble as I wedge them under the waistband of her jeans and trace it around to the front, before I open the top button and slide down the zipper. When she pulls down her jeans and steps out of them, my lips part in awe at the sight of her amazing body. Her white Calvin Klein crop top and briefs look like they were made for her, yet I'd rather see them come off too.

When I reach out to do just that, Syd takes back control, catching my wrist. She takes my other wrist too and pulls me closer, then studies me as my chest heaves up against hers. It's as if she's scanning every part of me, like a snake or a praying mantis, sizing up its next meal. I stand still, unsure if I'd be able to move even if I wanted to because the way she firmly holds me frightens and excites me at the same time. Her grip is strong, and I know I've just given away the last ounce of control, if I had any left in me. But when she claims my mouth again in a possessive kiss, I know I'm exactly where I'm supposed to be. She owns the place where all my secrets and darkest fantasies are hidden, and soon she's going to turn them into reality.

"You feel so good," Syd mumbles against my lips, still holding onto my wrists. She walks me toward the bed and when my legs hit the mattress, she lets go and unhooks my bra.

I shiver as she slides down the straps, letting it fall off me. There's no time to process what's happening as I'm suddenly pushed onto the bed and she crawls over me, enveloping one of my nipples with her warm mouth. I writhe underneath her and my hips jerk up. Why does it feel so good? I never liked it when Brian did this to me. Her tongue twirls around my hard bud before she bites down on it.

"Fuck..." My head falls back and my chest shoots up, begging for more. When she moves her knee between my legs and pushes it against my pussy, I let out a throaty moan at the rush of delight that courses through me. Even through my panties, I know she can feel how wet I am and that turns me on even more. I reach out to touch her in return, but again, she takes my wrists and places my hands above my head. Keeping them there with one hand, she bites her lip and shoots me a flirty smile, then continues to explore my breasts with her mouth. I'm delirious, wondering why I didn't come here sooner. The tugging of her teeth, the velvety touch of her tongue and her soft lips on my sensitive skin could send me over the edge right now and she knows it.

Syd lifts her head and looks at me, desire seeping through her gaze. She lets go of my hands and arches an eyebrow. "Don't move them unless I say you can."

I nod, unable to speak because her hands are now grabbing hold of my panties, sliding them down, exposing my waxed pussy. She gives me an approving look, the corners of her mouth tugging up as she licks her lips—hungry and ready to satisfy her appetite. I feel more exposed than ever and take in a quick breath as her eyes roam over me. My skin is so sensitive that I'm afraid I might come if she so much as blows on it.

"Spread your legs," she commands.

I swallow hard, thinking this is way more intense than on the video call. She's right in front of me, facing my most private parts and I'm at her mercy. Shaking with nerves and anticipation, I spread my legs that are still covered by my thigh-high hold-ups and watch her let out a soft whimper. "Perfect," she whispers, before getting down on her knees. "I'm going to make you scream. Would you like that?" Without waiting for an answer, she lowers herself to my pussy and laps at my juices, wedging her tongue between my over-sensitive folds.

"Aaaah!" My hips shoot up against her face and I have trouble keeping my hands where they are supposed to be as her skilled tongue brings me to the brink of an orgasm. Jesus, this woman really knows what she's doing and after only a couple of seconds, I feel like a volcano that's about to erupt.

Suddenly she pulls back and raises herself, studying me intently. The faint smile on her face tells me she likes my seismic reaction and she looks incredibly turned on herself, breathing fast with her lips slightly parted. They're glistening, covered in my juices, and when she licks them, I know I've never seen anything sexier in my life.

"Please don't stop," I whisper through ragged breaths, fighting the urge to move my hands and pull her back down.

Knowing what I'm about to do, Syd looks at my hands and shakes her head. "No... keep them right there." She crawls over me and lowers herself on top of me, sighing as our bodies come together. Her weight on me and her warm skin feel unbelievably good but when her hand strums down my body and settles between my legs, good is taken to a whole new level. I gasp when her fingers brush my clit before she enters me without warning, filling me up and making me cry out in ecstasy. Slowly, she starts fucking me, letting me get used to her while she rides my thigh. My moans come from deep within me, stifled by her mouth on mine. She kisses me with urgency, hard and deep like the way she penetrates me, faster now. All I can think is that I never want this to end, but very soon, our bodies tense up and we're both taken to greater heights.

"Look at me," Syd says when my eyes flutter closed as an orgasm of outrageous proportions rolls over me. "I want you to look at me while you..." She stops mid-sentence when she climaxes herself and when I look into her eyes, we share something so intense that no words can describe how I feel in those magic moments. When it fades, all I can do is continue to stare up into her captivating blue eyes. She's got me.

14

—————

"That was unbelievable," I say, noting I've rarely felt so relaxed before. My breathing is fast and my body still fluttering from the third orgasm she just gave me as I'm slowly coming back to my senses. Syd made good on her promise and made me scream over and over and if I had any doubt as to whether sex with a woman is for me, it's faded like it was never there.

"Good." Her lips trail featherlight kisses down my neck and she allows me to wrap my arms around her and run my hands through her hair. "Are you hungry?"

I almost laugh at that because the question comes out of nowhere and food is the last thing on my mind. As I listen to my stomach though, I realize that I am. I didn't eat much on the flight and my body's been in overdrive ever since.

"I am. Shall I order a pizza?" I ask.

"How about I take you out for dinner?"

"Okay..." I know I sound hesitant, but only because I didn't see this coming. I like to plan ahead, yet for some reason, I hadn't thought any further than the sex before I came here and suddenly, a dinner seems very intimate.

"Hey, it's not a date, it's dinner," Syd says as if reading my mind. She tilts her head and shoots me a cocky smile. There's no limit to her sexiness, and I find myself grinning as I agree.

"You're right. It's just dinner."

"Excellent." Syd gets up from the bed, still in her underwear. She throws me my dress and winks. "Nothing romantic, I promise."

With my dress in hand, I leave the room and head for the bathroom. I try the second door in the hallway, but it's locked. For a moment, I think about asking her what's in there, but that would be way too nosey. That door is probably locked for a reason and as long as she's not hiding a body, I don't care what's inside. Then a thought strikes me. What if she's got some kind of playroom or sex dungeon in there? I already know she likes toys—seeing as she's sent me two already—yet there's no trace of any sex paraphernalia anywhere in her bedroom. Is she waiting for the right moment to reveal her inner most secrets or is she figuring out how much I can handle? Or is she convinced that whatever is in that room is too much for me?

"If you're looking for the bathroom, it's the last door," Syd says, and I jump at the sound of her voice.

"Right. Thanks." I move on to the bathroom and lock myself in, taking deep breaths as I steady myself against the sink and stare at my reflection in the mirror. She caught me dawdling in front of the door, but there's nothing wrong with that, I tell myself. Anyone would be curious by a locked door but if I'm not meant to go in, I won't ask her about it.

I'm a little shocked at my appearance. My mascara has smudged, leaving dark marks under my brown, slightly dazed eyes and my hair is a mess. Still, I smile at myself, because I feel like a different person and I think I like the new me.

S yd pulls out a chair for me and I chuckle as I sit down. The cozy Italian restaurant is small and intimate. Waiters in black maneuver through the rows of tables in the candlelit dining space while Italian opera plays softly in the background.

"Nothing romantic, huh?" I say after a waiter has placed a bottle of water on our table and lit the candle now flickering between us.

"No. Just dinner." Syd shrugs and grins as if the situation amuses her. "It's close, and they have great food." She's right about the close part. The restaurant is under her apartment building and she's clearly familiar with the staff. The manager gave her a hug when we arrived and went through a lot of effort to place an extra table in the back for us. It's full, but our little corner feels private, and I'm glad we're not sitting in the middle of the room as we look like we're on a date. I put my black dress back on after a quick shower, and Syd looks jaw-droppingly attractive in jeans and a simple white shirt.

"Do you bring a lot of women here?" I ask casually, opening the menu.

"No. I'm pretty private and like my dates to be farther from home. But since you've already been in my bed and it doesn't get more private than that..."

I laugh, and I'm not sure if I believe her. Curiously, I find myself wanting to know more about her dating life. It's not that I'm jealous, and she's already told me she's single, but now that I'm here, and have had a glimpse of her life, I'd like to fill in the blanks. "Do you date a lot in general?"

"Not much, no." Syd shakes her head and smiles at the waiter, who brings over a bottle of red wine and pours us both a glass. "Do you want red, by the way?" she asks. "I apologize, I should have asked you, but I come here so often that I don't even think about it and they just assume..."

"No, red is great." I lean in too, craving the physical closeness from before already.

"Good." She takes a sip of her wine and closes her eyes for a beat, savoring the flavor. "Anyway, to answer your question properly, I don't date much. My girlfriend and I broke up last year and I haven't dated very much since. Occasionally, yes, but I haven't met a woman I've really clicked with yet."

I let her words sink in, wondering if she feels a click with me. I do feel like we connect, I suppose. I mean, I'm ridiculously attracted to her, but since she's a woman, I haven't thought beyond the sex and anyway, I haven't been looking for a relationship since my divorce. "How long were you together? You and your ex?"

"Talking about exes now, are we?" Syd regards me with interest, as if my questions have somehow added another layer to our purely sexual dynamic. She's not wrong. Until now, we haven't discussed much other than sex, but I decide I'd like to get to know her better. Besides, we're in a restaurant, so we can hardly discuss further plans for the night.

"Just curious."

"Six years," she finally says. "We grew apart over time, nothing dramatic. That and..." she pauses. "Well, let's just say that Adriana was never very interested in sex and I'm the opposite."

"I get that." I taste my wine and am surprised by how good the Malbec is; moreish and layered with a hint of clove. I consider myself a bit of a connoisseur and our common love for good wines was one of the few things that kept conversation flowing over dinner during my long and dull marriage. "In my case, I guess I was the one who wasn't that interested in sex."

"You didn't seem uninterested an hour ago." Syd grins. "So, maybe you like women and you didn't know. Or maybe it's just me who has that effect on you," she jokes. Her flirtatious tone turns me on, and I shift in my seat, my sensitive pussy a reminder of how she devoured me.

"Maybe. You're extremely talented in that department." I shake my head, because that statement doesn't nearly give her enough credit. "Actually, you deserve to know that that was the best sex I've ever had in my life."

"Thank you, I'll take that." She lowers her voice and adds: "We're not done yet. You know that, right? We're only just getting started."

"I know," I whisper, a blush creeping to my cheeks. I'm grateful for the waiter who comes to take our orders as I need distraction from my torrid fantasies that are threatening to take over my body. Scanning the menu, I note that I can't concentrate on anything at all, and leave it up to her. "You decide," I say, and close it again.

I observe Syd as she orders morel arancini, a fennel and blood orange salad and a lobster pasta dish to share. She's amicable with the waiter, joking and laughing with him in their native tongue and it only makes me like her more. My French is rusty, but I understand that they're talking about his girlfriend, who is a friend of Syd's.

Unlike LA, people seem real here. There's no chitchat for the sake of it, no fake compliments flying around, and the small-town girl in me, who I forgot about a long time ago, appreciates that.

"Done," Syd says, turning her attention back to me after

the waiter walks away with our order. "So, your turn. Why did you get divorced?" She hesitates. "If you don't mind me asking."

"No, I don't mind." I take a moment to think about my answer because there are probably a million reasons why Brian and I didn't work out. "I think it started after my first promotion. We were in our early twenties when we met, and we were both really ambitious. I've always worked in finance, and Brian was a software developer. He never said as much, but I always felt he didn't like that I had a better job than him and it was cause for a lot of friction between us. Brian likes to be top dog; he needs people to look up to him and I was never one of those people. Eventually, he started his own company and it was very successful. He worked long days and we hardly saw each other. Deep down, I knew he was having an affair, but I never asked him about it. I guess I just didn't care enough and one day, I decided I'd rather be on my own. His reaction didn't surprise me; he agreed immediately, but what I hoped would be an amicable divorce turned into an exhausting battle in court. I won't bore you with the details."

"That's sad." Syd tilts her head and her eyes burn into mine. "For what it's worth, Brian was crazy not to worship you and I happen to like strong, successful women."

"Thank you, that's nice of you to say." I pause and smile, letting her know I'm absolutely fine. "But life is good right now; I feel like I'm myself again, and I love living on my own. My friend Ellen keeps saying I should start dating but I don't feel like it."

"So you're not looking for a relationship?"

The question startles me, as I don't really know what I want from her and I'm afraid to give the wrong answer. "I wasn't," is all I can think of to say, and change the topic. "Tell me about your job."

Syd nods, understanding that's all she's getting. "My tattoo studio is two blocks from here. It's a shared space with a bunch of graphic designers and there's a decent café there too. My studio is my playroom, it's where I get creative three days a week, sometimes more if I have full-body work, and I'm lucky in that I have a waiting list so there's always work if I want it." I can tell she loves her job by the way her dazzling eyes light up. "I'd take you there but you're not here very long and I'm sure you'll agree that we can put our time to much better use."

I'm startled when I realize the waiter is beside me with our food. He places the plates between us and smirks at Syd, who doesn't seem to care that he's overheard our conversation. She starts plating up for me and takes great care in spooning out each dish as if it matters to her what I think about the food. There's a certain elegance and poise to the way she does things, and it contradicts her casual looks in the most fascinating way. Is she from a wealthy family? Not that I care, but her apartment in this quaint and highly popular neighborhood can't be cheap, and although I normally don't pay much attention in restaurants, as I don't have to worry about money myself, the hefty prices on the menu haven't gone unnoticed. She didn't just take me here to impress me; she's clearly a regular.

"You must do well as a tattoo artist to afford an apartment here." I'm not sure if it's out of order, but the words have escaped my mouth before I've had the time to think them through. Very unlike me, but then again, I'm all over the place right now, after having had mind-blowing, passionate sex with a woman for the first time in my life.

"I do all right." Syd pauses and regards me again. "But as I told you, I have many passions."

"Are you going to tell me about them?"

"Maybe. Not tonight, though." She spears a piece of arancini on her fork and holds it out in front of me. "Try it, it's heavenly."

I take a bite and am blown away by the exceptional flavor. It's so good that I have to close my eyes for a moment and savor the explosion in my mouth. "It's amazing," I say and for some reason, she fascinates me even more now. Although I can't stand not knowing things—I'm not one for surprises—the mystery that surrounds her also intrigues me, and it's very attractive.

"Told you so." She looks pleased with herself as she settles her eyes on mine again. "So, what about your passions, Val?"

15

It's late by the time we get back and I'm both restless with pent-up sexual energy and giddy with excitement because I've had a truly great night. Syd is interesting, funny, kind and chivalrous, and that last one takes a little getting used to. It was strange to have her get the check and help me into my coat, but it also made me feel special and appreciated. I'm not sure what I envisioned but being treated like a lady by another woman certainly wasn't one of my expectations before I came here.

She closes the door behind us and takes my coat before removing her own. Her smile is infectious, and I know she's had a good time too. I want more of her but most of all, I want to please her, taste her, drive her wild like she did to me earlier. We stare at each other for a beat, the heat between us reigniting now that we're alone again.

"Would you like another coffee?" she asks, taking a step toward me. She runs a hand through my hair, cups my neck and pulls me in for a kiss that is slow and sensual. A moan passes our lips and I'm still truly amazed by how good it feels to make out with her. My hungry mouth deepens the kiss and I reach out to unbutton her shirt.

"No," I mumble, and feeling bold, I add: "I want you. Let me have you instead."

Syd pulls out of the kiss and shoots me a cheeky grin as if she knew this moment would come. She's planned this carefully; driving me insane with lust since I arrived, yet she's letting me take my time, gently easing me into this.

In the bedroom, she undresses me and lets me undress her too. We're slow, as if we're exploring together, and knowing what's coming next, my one-track mind is going places I can't quite handle yet. A little more relaxed after the wine over dinner, I'm braver this time though, and can't wait to see her naked. I'm lost for words as I take off her crop top and stare at her breasts. They're small and full, with perfect pink nipples; hard and inviting. I want to touch them, but my hands feel clumsy.

Taking charge, Syd takes my hand and guides it to one of her breasts. Holding my breath, I slide my fingers over the taut nipple, then around the beautiful curve, cupping it as I lean in to kiss her. It feels phenomenal, and my other hand joins in, taking in her softness and feminine curves. As I stop thinking and let my body do what it wants to do, my movements become natural, and we fall into a dance of pushing and pulling, giving and taking. Exploring her ribcage, the curve of her waist, her toned arms, her shoulder blades and her trim stomach that tenses up when I run my fingers over it, I know that this is what I truly want. I'm getting to know her, and at the same time, I'm getting to know myself.

My thumbs hook under the elastic edge of her briefs and I pull them down over her hips. Seeing her naked on camera aroused me, but this is a whole different thing. It's thrilling to have her right in front of me, to be able to touch her.

Her hand catches mine again and she guides it between her thighs. I quiver as I touch her carefully, moving my fingers down the thin strip of dark hair. When I brush my finger over her engorged clit, she gasps, her hips jerking in reflex.

"Does that feel good?" I whisper, marveling at her expression of utter delight. Her breath quickens and she looks like she's losing control.

"You have no idea." Syd places her hand over mine and pushes it lower, where my fingers find a pool of liquid desire. It drives me crazy to know I do this to her, and I slide my hand farther, my breath hitching at the wetness that coats my fingertips. Taking my time, I explore her as we kiss, and I listen to the sounds she makes, slowly learning what she likes. I'm so turned on just by touching her that my pussy aches, and overcome with desire, I slide a fingertip inside her.

Syd gasps against my mouth and starts kissing me with more urgency. It gives me confidence and I cup her ass and pull her closer as I enter her deeper, then add another finger. My movements make her back up against the chair by the vanity table, and she moves it away, then sits down on top of the table. Its old frame is sturdy, and it doesn't give way when I spread her legs and move between them to fuck her while I kiss her wildly. We're both on the brink of losing it as she wraps her legs around mine. The smell of the lilies in the vase right next to us stirs the back of my mind, and I know I'll always associate them with this moment. I feel powerful as her pleasure grows, knowing there's no way she can stop it.

It's not enough for me though, as I want all of her now.

She shoots me a heated glance when I pull out and kneel down between her thighs. Her natural scent is intoxicating, the sight of her naked sex and her musky aroma stupefying me. I put my hands on her thighs to push them farther apart and don't hesitate to slowly run my tongue over her sex. She jerks her hips when I reach her clit and she tastes so good that I bury myself in her heat. Shuddering with every lap of my tongue, Syd groans and throws her head back, her hands moving into my hair to pull me closer. I drive my tongue inside her, and when she suddenly explodes, much faster than I thought she would, I can feel her contractions like she's trying to suck me in. It triggers something salacious in me, blows my mind to dust, and I moan against her delicious pussy, digging my nails into her behind, so hard I'm afraid I might have hurt her.

"Val..." Syd whispers as she tips my chin up. She looks bewildered and opens her mouth to speak, but no words come from her lips, as if she's too blown to say anything. Then she shakes her head and bites her lip with an amused smirk, pulling me up so I'm standing before her.

"Was that okay?" I ask, smiling smugly because I think I already know the answer.

"That was..." She laughs, continuing to shake her head. "Let's just say I think we're a perfect match."

"I'll take that as a yes." I lean in to touch her face, drowning in her eyes that look at me as if I'm all she's ever wanted.

16

I feel surprisingly languid when my eyes flutter open, and sigh deeply at Syd's warm body against mine. She's spooning me; her arm is wrapped around my waist and her face is nuzzling my neck. It feels strange, but only because it's different to waking up with a man, and that's a good thing, I decide. The silky smoothness of her skin, her sweet scent, the sound of her soft breathing while she sleeps... It's all so heavenly and endearing.

My body is deliciously sore and tired, and I can feel where she's been, the slight ache in my pussy reminding me of everything she's done to me. Yesterday was beyond amazing, and I'm glad I still have another night to enjoy my new favorite pastime. Fleeting thoughts about my sexuality enter my mind but none of it really matters. If I'm gay, so be it. It's not like they're going to fire me at work, and my parents might even get over it too, if I choose to tell them. Over the course of the past sixteen hours, it's become pretty clear that I prefer women though, at least one woman in particular.

I hadn't anticipated the wonderful conversations over dinner and waking up in her arms but I'm incredibly comfortable around her. On a whim that is highly out of character for me, I turn around and take her in my arms, pressing my body tighter against hers. Waking up slowly, she responds to my display of affection by wedging a leg between my thighs and embracing me too, pulling me in. It feels divine, but aware of what I've just done—my body instantly reacting to her touch–my pulse starts racing. Is it too much? It seemed like the natural thing to do, because we fit together perfectly, our limbs easily falling into place like pieces of a puzzle.

"Good morning, princess," she mumbles against my shoulder.

"Good morning." I allow myself to indulge in her eyes as she looks up and blinks against the beam of sunlight that's pouring through the gap in the curtains. "Sorry if I woke you up."

Syd shakes her head and smiles, making me melt all over again. "Thank you for doing so." Her hand moves over my ass and gives it a squeeze. "We shouldn't be wasting any time..." At that, she rolls on top of me and kisses me deep. Her weight on me and her tongue claiming my mouth make me squirm as she grinds into me hard. Jesus. This woman is unbelievable, the way she brings me to the edge of a climax in a matter of seconds.

Syd knows I'm close already and I think she feels pleased about it as she stops and lifts her head to study my expression that I know is nothing short of delirious. Her face looks adorably sleepy, but I know she's wide awake now, turned on by my need.

"Don't stop." I spread my legs farther, begging her to continue.

"Wait." She rolls over, opens her nightstand drawer and takes something out. When I see what it is, I swallow hard, my eyes widening in surprise. It's not like I hadn't expected her to have a strap-on, following our video calls, but seeing her step into the straps and attach the dildo as if it's the most common thing in the world, is something else altogether. My clit twitches and arousal pulses through me when she lowers herself on top of me again. "Are you okay with trying this?"

I nod, and gasp when she slowly starts entering me, sliding in, inch by inch. My body stretches to accommodate her, and it isn't painful but rather exquisite, like we're becoming one. My pussy is pulsing, gripping onto the shaft as she starts fucking me slowly and lazily like the sleepy state that we're in. Sex with Syd is like a really great, complex wine. After the first burst of indulgent harmonious flavors comes the depth, then hints of unexpected ingredients; a surprise, like with a red Burgundy or a Barolo, and it only gets better as you dig deeper into your palate and give into its finesse. I'm in heaven, and I can see she is too. We move in sync, my legs wrapped around her hips and my hands in her hair. We kiss, and she moans against my lips, opening my mouth with her tongue. She's mercifully sinking into me again and again. The dildo is repeatedly brushing up against my clit, and a few strokes later I'm about to explode. I don't need to tell her; she can feel it by my hands moving to her back, gripping her tighter and tighter, and I know she's close by her quick breaths and her rapid heartbeat against my chest. When her moans become louder, she moves a hand between us, rubbing my clit until I tense up and force my eyes open to look at her. She nods, and we're both swept away in a tidal wave of pleasure, drowning in bliss, bucking, thrashing, shuddering against each other. I hold her, not wanting it to end, because this is everything to me. This, right now, is what it feels like to be alive.

"Why did you not bring this out last night?" I ask when I'm lying in her arms a little later. "I was wondering where you kept your toys."

Syd tilts her head and smiles, stroking my hair. "I didn't want to frighten you. You told me you'd never been with a woman before, so I wanted to... I don't know... ease you into it, I suppose. Having sex with someone in real life is a whole different thing than watching each other get off online."

I laugh. "I'm not sure if easing into it justifies what you did to me last night. It was rather explosive." I pause. "But yes, I get that. Thank you, for being so thoughtful, I feel very comfortable with you."

"Good." Syd lets out a deep sigh as she pulls me in closer. "And for the record, I don't tend to keep my toys in the nightstand drawer. I have a few, though."

"So where are they?" I ask, playful and curious. "Are they in the room next door?" My mind goes back to the locked door, imagining a red painted room with a big, leather bed, whips, floggers, vibrators and everything else I love reading about.

Syd chuckles and shrugs, as she brings her lips close to mine again. "Maybe. You'll just have to wait and see."

17

———

"Stay here." Syd kisses me and rolls out of bed to put on a robe. "I'm going to make you breakfast." Tightening the tie, she gives me a flirty wink over her shoulder.

"Could you be any more perfect?" I ask playfully, arching an eyebrow at her. Seventeen years with Brian and never once did I get breakfast in bed. It almost frightens me how great she is, and I hate to admit it, but I don't really want to leave again so soon. This is way too good to just give up and I'm starting to wonder where we will go from here. Is this just a onetime thing for her? It was for me, initially. I wanted to explore my sexuality, know if it really was as good as I thought it would be. Truth is, it's way better, and I don't want it to end just yet. Shaking it off, I reach for my phone in my purse next to the bed, telling myself we still have time. I laugh when I see I have six messages from Ellen:

17:03: 'How is she?'

18:45: 'Have you had sex yet?'

20:23: 'What's it like to feel a woman's boobs?'

23:59: 'Hey! Don't ignore me, you promised to let me in on every detail.'

08:30: 'Why aren't you answering me? Has she tied you up in her dungeon?'

09:45: 'Seriously, Val. I'm worried. Call me or I'll alert the cops.'

The last message was sent twenty minutes ago so I quickly reply, knowing she probably will call the cops if I don't answer. I've been so pleasantly preoccupied with Syd that I haven't even looked at my phone, which is very rare for me.

'Sorry was busy >wink<. I'm safe and it's been amazing. BTW the wine here is incredible, so snob all you want .' Of course, my phone immediately lights up again, but I throw it back in my purse as I just want to sit here and enjoy myself for a little while longer.

The sun is shining brightly, and I jump out of bed to open the French doors that are connected to the same balcony adjacent to the living room, then crawl back under the covers. It's not so chilly today, and the fresh air and sunshine on my face makes me smile. Syd's bedroom suddenly seems terribly romantic, with the antique four poster bed, the old furniture and open French doors over-looking the same beautiful redbrick buildings on the other side of the road. It's got a Parisian vibe to it, and I chuckle to myself, knowing Ellen couldn't have been more wrong about this city.

Syd comes back with a large tray that she places on the bed. I feel butterflies well up inside me when I see the red rose lying between two enormous cappuccinos, and the plates with poached eggs and avocado on toast. Truth be told, it brings a lump to my throat because she is so thoughtful and sweet, and I'm not used to that. The idea that this is just about sex for her is slowly starting to evaporate and the way I see her is starting to change, too. I love being with her and I love how she makes me feel. Although we've been communicating online with each other for over two months, meeting in person has changed everything, and given me so much to think about.

"Are you okay? Is it too much?" she asks jokingly, but I can see that she's worried it might be.

"No, it's sweet." My eyes meet hers and I feel like I want to hug her. "You're so sweet... and unexpectedly romantic."

"I'm not." She shrugs. "I just like making you smile, and I noticed from your reaction in the restaurant last night that you're not used to being treated the way you deserve to be treated. I think it's time that changes, don't you?"

"I'm not complaining. I don't think I could come up with a more perfect way of waking up. Especially not after what you just did to me..." I blush and focus on my coffee, aware that she's watching me.

"Couldn't agree more." Syd grins. "I like waking up like this too."

"Are you not working today?" I ask.

"No. You're here." The way she says it makes it sound like that's a given. "I thought maybe we could go for a walk if you're up for it."

"A walk sounds nice," I say, and try to remember when I last did that. "People don't go for walks in LA."

"I know. I've been there a couple of times." She gives me a knowing look. "Where are you from originally?"

"Oregon. A small town called Silverton."

"That sounds nice. Do you go back a lot?"

"Not much. My parents still live there so I visit them over

Christmas, and they come to see me in LA once a year. I don't have any siblings."

"And you never had children..." Syd flinches. "Sorry, is that too personal to ask about?"

"No, it's fine. My career always came first, I suppose. Brian never wanted children either, and by the time he changed his mind and started bringing it up, our marriage was already falling apart so I'm glad we didn't go there in the end." I shrug. "And now, I'm finally happy just by myself. What about you? Are you from here?"

Syd nods as she sips her coffee. "Born and bred. My parents still live here, and I have two older brothers who are both in Quebec too. I travelled a lot when I was younger, looking for a better place or a change." She shrugs. "Or maybe I was just looking for myself, who knows? I never found anywhere where I felt happier though, so I came back and never left after that."

"Kids?"

"No. I would have told you by now if I had kids."

"Of course." I purse my lips, wondering if I'm firing off too many questions. "Why do you sound so American? I noticed most people here have a French accent when they speak English, but you don't. I assume the school system isn't bilingual?"

"No, but my father is American, so we spoke English at home, and I studied in Washington. Art history and literature," Syd adds. "I couldn't get enough of college, so I went for two degrees." She laughs. "Must have been all the pretty girls there."

"And then you ended up being a tattoo artist?" I quickly wave a hand when I recognize how that must have sounded. "I didn't mean to insinuate that being a tattoo artist isn't a good career choice, it just seems an unusual one for someone who's highly educated."

"Maybe. But inking is a form of art too. I combine what I've learned with what inspires me to create my designs, and I want them to be meaningful. I'm interested in knowing things, but I never had a desire to work in commerce. I just want to have fun, and teaching or sitting in an office is not my idea of fun." She chuckles and shoots me an apologetic look. "No offence, I think it's super sexy that you're high up in a big company and working in finance obviously suits you, but it's not for me and I doubt it ever will be."

I laugh, not taking offence in the slightest. "Each to their own. I like my job but yes, I get why you're not into the corporate vibe. It's not for everyone and it can suck the life out of you if you let work overtake your life. That used to happen to me sometimes, but since my divorce I'm enjoying life more; I let go when I get home now and focus on other things." I chuckle. "Like reading lesbian erotica and calling you every night."

We eat our breakfast and talk about our parents and it seems so normal to sit here in bed with her, sharing personal stories. The bedroom door is open, and I keep glancing into the hallway, thinking of that locked room. I remind myself that it's none of my business, that she doesn't owe me an explanation, yet I can't help wondering what lies behind it.

"Tell me, Syd, because I just have to know. Is your sex dungeon in that room?"

"What? The one that's locked? You really can't let it go, can you?" Syd laughs and shakes her head. "Not quite. But it is the place where all my fantasies come true." She decides to leave it at that, and now my curiosity has gone through the roof.

"That sounds intriguing."

Syd frowns and bites her lip, and I silently hope she's going to tell me after all. But then she shakes her head and laughs it off. "Believe me, it's not what you think." Changing the subject, she asks: "Want to have a shower with me?"

18

We walk down Rue du Petit-Champlain, where she lives, and enter a maze of narrow streets, passing beautiful churches, galleries, courtyards and quaint shops inside the walled city. The old cobblestone streets are a little hard to master on my heels, so I buy a pair of black lacquered loafers that look decent with my black slacks and red, silk blouse. When I change my shoes, Syd is taller than me and it's nice when she wraps her arm around me and pulls me in.

As we meander down the antique and art district in the lower town, she acts as tourist guide, giving me a brief overview of the history and architecture of the city. She's clearly passionate and highly knowledgeable about her home city, and I absorb everything she tells me like a sponge. She's fascinating to listen to, and even more fascinating to look at. Her jeans and old ragged gray sweater accentuate the carefree, sexy tomboyish vibe she gives off and, as we walk, I can see other women eyeing her up, perhaps envying me.

"I like your city," I say. "It reminds me of Paris; I lived there a year, for work."

"Is that why you speak French? I heard you talking to the sales lady in the shoe store. It's pretty impressive, not many Americans speak French."

I laugh. "It's hardly impressive. But I get by just enough to survive, and I understand a little."

Syd nods, and listens intently as I tell her about my time there. It was before I met Brian, my second year in my first job. Everything was so exciting back then, and I think of it fondly. She seems genuinely interested in my stories, and asks me lots of questions, taking my hand while we walk. It's nice to just walk and talk; it's simple, relaxing, and holding her hand is definitely something I could get used to. The way her thumb lightly brushes my skin, letting me know she appreciates the contact. I'm not uncomfortable in public with her. Quite the opposite; I'm proud to be by her side and it's nice to feel close to someone again.

"I like LA too," Syd says as we sit down for a coffee. "It's not somewhere I'd necessarily want to live, but it's fun and I'm a big fan of sunny beaches."

"Then maybe you should come and visit me in return." I feel myself blush as I say it and I'm aware of the goofy grin that's plastered all over my face.

"I'd like that." She stretches her long legs out under the table and brushes a foot along my calf. The way she flirts with me sends me insane, and I can't get enough of her touch. "So, was that an invite?"

"It was."

"Good. Because you know I'll come." Her blue eyes lock with mine and I know I could sit here and stare into them forever. "I really like you, Val."

"I really like you too," I say, and realize we need to talk about this. "Maybe it's a little early for this conversation, but what are we actually doing? I didn't expect this to be anything more than sex." I hesitate. "But I'm having a really good time with you. In and out of bed."

"Me too. And I want to see you again." Syd's expression turns serious. "I feel like we click. Technically, we couldn't be more different, but we seem to work naturally, you know? I never really thought of anything beyond sex either, especially since you told me you were straight." She arches an eyebrow. "Or at least you thought you were, but I'm not so sure about that."

"No, you're right. I'm not so sure anymore either. Whatever I am, the lines have definitely blurred." I would never have doubted my sexuality if I hadn't met Syd and I would have put my love of lesbian erotica books down to some weird fetish. But I did meet her, and here I am. "Why did you approach me online?" I ask, even though I've asked the same question before.

"I found you attractive. Your profile picture, I mean," Syd clarifies. "And we read the same books. When you told me about your favorite Sadie London book, that kind of turned me on, so I wanted to chat to you in private." She bites her lip and pauses for a moment before she continues. "Sadie London writes about a lot of things we haven't done together."

I take in a quick breath and my lips part as I process what she's saying. "Yes, she does." My words are a near whisper, and I feel my body heat up, arousal coursing through my veins.

"Have you ever been tied up before?" She asks then, lowering her voice. The coffee shop is busy, and I look around to make sure no one is listening in.

"No." There's a long silence between us in which we're undoubtedly having the same indecent fantasies.

"Would you like me to tie you up?" Syd's eyes never leave

mine during our steamy exchange, her profound stare setting me on fire, and at the same time scaring the hell out of me.

"Yes," I whisper, trying to control my breathing. The thought of being at Syd's mercy—submissive and yielding to her touch—turns me on like nothing ever has. I've read about bondage, fantasized about it, but I never thought I'd be in the position where I'd consider it, and even agree to it. It's as if we have an understanding now, and silent communication passes between us until she finally speaks again.

"Do you trust me?"

"Yes." I shift in my seat, thinking I should really respond with something other than a monosyllabic answer. "Even though I don't really know you..." I pause and take a deep breath. "Yeah, I trust you."

"Good." Syd licks her lips, her eyes lighting up as her mind goes elsewhere, distracted for a beat before she snaps back. "Then that's what I'll do. Tonight."

19

After a wonderful walk and a couple of stops for coffee and lunch, we get back late in the afternoon. There's tension in the air as we step into her apartment, but of the good kind, and after our talk, that was hours ago by now, my body is tight with anticipation.

Syd seems kind of self-conscious too, as we linger in the hallway. "I haven't been entirely honest with you," she says out of nowhere.

"What?" My eyes narrow in confusion as I observe her. Syd's made me swoon, I've given myself to her and I've been nothing but open, and now she's telling me there's something I should know? I'm not sure I like where this is heading. My mind and body are on high alert as she sorts through her key ring, presumably looking for the key that opens the door. "What do you mean?"

"When you told me you'd never been with a woman before... that was probably the right time to tell you I had a secret too, but I didn't and I'm sorry about that." Syd looks at me intently. "I had to meet you first because I wasn't sure if I could trust you, so I really hope you understand because what I'm about to show you needs to stay between us." She takes my hand as if preparing me for what I'm about to see and now I'm seriously getting worried that there might actually be a person in there, shackled to the wall. "But if we're going to do what we discussed," she continues, "there has to be mutual trust and you need to know the important stuff about me too."

When she unlocks the door, I hold my breath as I enter and prepare myself for anything. Nothing could have surprised me more though, when Syd switches on the light and shows me a rather dull looking office. There's a storage cupboard, desk, a leather office chair, a laptop and shelves full of books. A couple of boxes are stacked up against the back wall but other than that, there are only a bunch of plants and some framed photographs on the walls.

"I don't understand... Why do you keep this locked?"

Syd nods toward the bookshelves. "Look closer."

I walk past the rows of books on the wall-mounted shelves and see that they're all Sadie London books. She has at least five copies of each title, which is a little weird. Then I notice the framed pictures are book covers, also by Sadie London. "Is this some kind of shrine? Are you obsessed with her?" I ask. "Because as much as I like her books, even I'm a little uncomfortable seeing this."

Syd laughs and shakes her head. "No, I'm not obsessed. But you like her books, right? Within the genre anyway," she adds. "I have no idea what else you read."

I nod, confused as to where this conversation is going.

"Well, the thing is... I'm Sadie London."

There's a silence while I process what she's telling me. Is she making this up? But then why would she do that? "You?" I ask incredulously.

"Yes. I use the book clubs to get honest opinions on my

books. I'm a member of a couple, I have been for years. Sadie London is my pen name and Sydney Heller is my real name, which I use for the chat groups." Syd looks worried as she fixes her eyes with mine. "But I never expected to meet someone like you on there."

At that, I tilt my head and my lips pull into a small smile. I understand why she couldn't tell me; I wouldn't trust my secret with someone I've never met before either. It still takes a moment before it sinks in that Syd's the reason I started reading lesbian erotica in the first place, and I'm now in her apartment, after what can only be described as the best night of my life. It's like fate threw me into this situation. "It's okay," I finally say. "I get why you didn't tell me, but I'm glad you have now. So, you're really Sadie London?" Now there's another big question on my mind—one that I need to know the answer to. "Do you make a habit of having sex with your readers?"

"No, I never do this." She points between us and something about her voice tells me she's speaking the truth. "Only with you. No one apart from my parents, brothers and a handful of friends know I write, and I never invite people I don't know into my private space. But with you... I guess I had a good feeling about you, and I couldn't exactly put you up in a hotel now, could I?"

I feel honoured that I'm one of the few to know this about her, but then more questions enter my mind. "When you said you needed to get inspired... Have you been using me for research purposes?"

"No, I've been using you for my pleasure, just like you've been using me for yours. And yes, you've inspired me—I mean, how could you not—but there's nothing wrong with getting inspired by pleasure."

I nod because she has a point. I've had more pleasure

these past twenty-four hours than I can handle and frankly, I've never felt so sexually satisfied. It also doesn't help that I find her more fascinating now, and my head can't seem to stop replaying the steamy chapters I've read over and over, knowing that they came from her mind. They're her thoughts, her fantasies, and I'm here to make them come true. "Okay. Your secret is safe with me," I say, lowering my gaze to her lips. I want to kiss her, but something tells me I should wait. It's like there's been an even bigger power shift and I feel like I need to leave everything up to her from here on in.

"Thank you." Syd lets out a deep sigh of relief and shoots me a grateful glance. "I'm glad you understand." Her eyes darken, and she licks her lips, no doubt a lot of things running through her mind, now that we've got this out of the way. For a moment, I think she's going to take me right there and then, but instead she composes herself and opens the storage cupboard taking out a large, black box. "Are you ready to go into the bedroom?"

20

I'm lying down in the middle of the bed, listening to my own heartbeat. My pulse is racing; I can feel the vein in my neck pumping with adrenaline. Syd has stripped me down and I'm only wearing my black, lace panties. We haven't kissed and other than undressing me, she hasn't touched me. Syd, who is still fully clothed, is calm and seems to know exactly what she's doing. I watch her place the black box on the floor next to the bed and take out two leather cuffs with a piece of long rope hooked through a D-ring on top of the strap.

"May I?" It's the first thing she's said to me since we entered the bedroom. Everything happened in silence, and it's like we're partaking in some secret ritual. "If you want me to stop at any point, just say 'red' and I'll untie you immediately, okay? I'm not going to hurt you. I just want to find out what you like."

I nod and hold out my hand, allowing her to lock me in the buckled cuff and then secure my arm to the bedpost. Then she walks around the bed and repeats the action before giving the rope a quick final tug. She steps back, taking me in and I can see that she's incredibly turned on by me lying here naked and with my arms spread wide. I am too, and my heart starts pounding even faster when I realize I can't free myself.

"Are you okay?" Syd strokes my face and looks into my eyes.

"Yes." I sound like I'm out of breath, my chest is rising and falling fast. I'm trapped, but I know she'll let me go if I tell her to. An ache starts in my pussy when I see she has two more cuffs, but for now, she just places them on the bed next to me, so I can get used to the idea, I assume. She looks me over once more and reaches out to run her hand over my breasts. Never taking her eyes off mine, she pinches one of my nipples and holds it, then pinches harder until I flinch and suck in a quick breath through my teeth. My eyes are wide with surprise and I'm trying to figure out whether I like it or not. I think I do, because I want her to do it again.

Syd repeats the action with my other nipple, and now that I know what to expect, the reward is a flash of heat that strikes me between my legs, making me moan. She doesn't ask me if I like it; she can tell by my reaction that I do. Her hand slides down over my ribcage and my belly, then stops at the edge of my panties. I jerk my hips up, wanting her to continue, but she simply smiles and steps away, pleased with my reaction to her teasing.

Reaching into the box again, she takes out a brand-new black riding crop, removes it from the packaging and holds it up for me to see.

Again, my body reacts with a feverish need and I nod, letting her know I want this—or at least I want to find out if I do. The soft leather of the crop tickles my skin as she traces it along my face and neck, then over my collarbone and my breasts, teasing my nipples. I'm in two minds; loving the rush of arousal its touch gives me but also scared of what's to come. Just when I start easing into the caress of the crop, thinking this is going to be simple, she rapidly raises it and strikes the side of my breast. My chest shoots up and I take in a quick breath, tugging at my restraints. Instinctively, I want to put my hand there to protect myself but my bindings prevent that. It doesn't really hurt, but I hadn't expected it and so I tense up, preparing myself for the next strike. Syd stops to take me in, decides I'm okay and does it once more, a little harder this time.

"Fuck!" I yelp, more out of shock than pain. It stings a little, but it's a nice sting that leaves a warm glow on my breast. I note that I'm highly turned on and my pussy is dripping wet. I like this.

"Hold it." Syd places the crop between my teeth and it's a little uncomfortable, but I like the taste of fresh leather against my tongue. She moves along the bed to slowly pull down my panties, her movements careful, handling me like I'm a porcelain doll. The thought of her seeing how wet I am makes me quiver and another silent moan escapes my mouth when she stares between my legs, the corners of her mouth tugging upward. She tosses my panties on the floor and bends over me before she takes the crop back, reflecting my thoughts: "You're so into this."

Even though she's right, I don't manage to answer. A strange mixture of delight, shock and anticipation have taken away my ability to think straight. It's like I'm only my body now, only my impulse.

Continuing to tease, Syd draws the crop down my body so slowly I can barely feel it move. When it reaches my belly button, she drags it to my hip, then over my thigh, leaving a trail of goose bumps on my skin. "Spread your legs," she says, tapping me on my thigh. When I don't immediately comply, she strikes me there twice in quick succession, making me gasp. I spread my legs a little, and then she brings it down even harder on the inside of my right thigh. "Wider."

My legs are shaky as I submit to her command, and I feel exposed and vulnerable. My nerve endings are on high alert and it's like every touch is so much more extreme and impactful. My pussy is begging for attention, my clit twitching and aching it's so hard.

Syd places the crop between my teeth again and picks up the other two cuffs. "Are you still okay?"

This is clearly a question she wants an answer to, and I nod as I'm unable to speak with the crop in my mouth. Syd takes one of my ankles and secures it to the bedpost. She's careful, almost tender, the way she caresses it before tightening the cuff. When she takes my other foot, I freeze as my legs stretch wider apart, leaving me completely at her mercy.

Walking around the bed, she takes me in. "God, you have no idea how fucking sexy you look right now." I could say the same for her because the look in her eyes drives me wild as she roams her gaze over my body, looking down and then back up again. She takes the crop and trails it up the inside of my leg until I'm so ready that I can't take it anymore.

"Higher... please," I mutter, tilting my head from side to side.

"Higher?" Syd brings it down hard, striking my pussy with force. I cry out and levitate off the bed, my body convulsing with both pleasure and pain. The sensation is profound and makes me feel alive, the sharp sting shooting right through to my inner core. "You mean there?" she asks, licking her lips. Her voice is teasing, and I can hear that she's enjoying my whimpers as a glowing sensation settles on my sore pussy lips. I hardly have time to recover before she does it again.

"Fuck!" My head falls back and my eyes close tight.

"Want me to stop?" Syd walks over to me, cups my face and kisses me hard. Then she pulls away and lifts my chin for me to look at her. "Or do you want one more before I give you what you need?" Her expression is not sadistic, she knows it makes me feel good and she wants to finish what we started. I'm so close to coming and I'm not sure how much more I can take before I fall over the edge and climax. "You have to ask for more. I'm not doing anything you don't want me to do."

"One more," I say, barely in a whisper, and I close my eyes again, preparing myself for the crop. It comes down hard, but the flash of pain is immediately taken over by a warm and wet sensation that feels so sublime, I can barely contain myself as I cry out her name. "Syd! Fuck!" I come with a force that almost scares me, and it doesn't seem to end. I have no idea what's going on but when I look down, I see she has crawled between my legs and her mouth is on me. She grabs my hips and drinks me in, all of me. It's so powerful that my toes curl and my hands ball into fists, the cuffs chafing my wrists as my nails dig hard into my own skin. Thrusting my hips against her hungry mouth, I moan as she sucks the last aftershocks out of me. It leaves me throbbing, trembling, speechless, and more than a little confused. What the hell just happened? I mean, I know what happened, but if felt surreal, like I was looking down on myself. She's touched a sacred part inside of me and it's opened up portals I never knew existed. My body is in a state of bliss, all my muscles loose and limp as I lie here, unable to tear my gaze away from Syd, whose face is still buried between my thighs.

She looks up, gives me a sexy smile and licks her lips like a cat after finishing its meal. There's something feline about her; the way she moves and does things with so much grace, always controlled, never in a rush. "Good?"

"Uhuh." My ability to form a sentence has not returned yet, and I think it might be a while before I'm able to say something that makes sense. I follow her with my eyes as she undresses on the bed, salivating at the sight of her naked form. She crawls up and straddles me, then brushes her lips against mine before claiming my mouth. Kissing her and tasting myself on her lips feels incredible and I want to wrap my arms around her, but I can't.

"Not yet," she says, raising herself with a twinkle in her eyes. She grabs two pillows from the bed and places them on my arms. I can't work out what she's planning to do but then she moves forward, kneeling in front of my face with a leg on each side. I can smell her arousal, see her glistening wetness. When she lowers herself down to my mouth, I lap at her divine juices, cherishing her flavor. The sounds she makes and the way she rotates her hips over me drive me wild and I'm immediately turned on again. I take her throbbing clit into my mouth and suck it hard until she starts shaking, moaning louder. It's incredible to have this power over her, even though I'm tied up, and I feel euphoric when she lets out a loud cry, arching her back as she holds onto the bedframe.

Syd stays there, catching her breath until finally, she relaxes and crawls off me, then reverently unbuckles my wrists and ankles. She lies down beside me and we fall into an embrace, our limbs entangled, holding onto each other like we never want to let go. I let out a soft sigh against her neck, marveling at how close I feel to her. Overcome with feelings I barely understand, I know one thing for certain: I don't want this to end.

21

Syd strokes my dark hair and smiles at me. "I'm not sure how you feel about leaving the bed, but I'm thirsty and hungry."

"Yeah, me too." I want to stay here but my stomach is rumbling and I'm a little light-headed after four hours of exploring my sexual proclivities and finding out the most astonishing things about myself. Syd doesn't push me, but I'm curious and I want to know everything, now that I've had a taste of how good sex can be. "I can cook you something if you have ingredients in the house." It sounds strange coming from my mouth as I don't think I've uttered those words before. I don't even like to cook but I desperately want to do something for her in return.

"No, you're my guest and you look like you need a rest. How about burgers, fries and a bath?" Syd grins and reaches for her phone. "We need to keep our strength up. I'll order them." She opens a delivery app and hands it to me. "You pick, unless you prefer something else? It's a shame to get dressed if we have so little time left..." Her remark leaves a thick silence between us, and we look at each other, knowing we're thinking the same thing: This cannot be the end.

"Burgers sound great," I mumble, melancholy settling in my stomach at the prospect of flying back to LA tomorrow.

C andles are flickering under the mirror in Syd's small bathroom and foam is cascading over the edge of the tub as we sit down, each on one side. There's a folding table next to the bathtub with our food, a bottle of water and two glasses of white wine. We've been quiet until the delivery arrived, just cherishing each other's company as we held each other in bed, but now I have so many questions, hopes and doubts.

"So, you're really coming to visit me?"

Syd nods while she chews her food, never taking her eyes off me. "Of course. If you want that."

"I do." I sink down deeper in the water, resting my feet against the other end of the tub, clutching her waist. "Coming here, I didn't think it would be so..." I take my time to find the right words but fail.

"Intense?" Syd finishes my sentence. "Amazing, surprising, mind-blowing, phenomenal, thrilling, insightful... passionate?"

"Yes, all of that." I swallow hard, gathering courage to speak my mind. "I had no expectations apart from hoping we'd have great sex. But I really like you, and honestly, I think I'm going to miss you..." I bite my lip and hesitate. "So I want to thank you for two wonderful days." What I really want to tell her, is that the past two days have been life-altering, but I figure that might be a bit much, even though it feels that way.

"The pleasure was all mine." Syd studies me intently

and takes a sip of her wine. "I sense you're sad, but this doesn't have to be the end, Val. It can be more than just the occasional visit if you want it to be. There's nothing complicated about our situation other than the fact that we live far apart." She shrugs. "A lot of people live far apart, and they manage to make it work."

Her words cover me with comfort like the warm water we're immersed in. "What are you saying?" I feel a glimmer of hope and manage a smile. I'm never this melodramatic and I don't understand how I got this way just by being in her presence. But Syd has something magical about her, a way of reeling me in and making me love her world and her mind, and I don't want to lose that.

"I'm saying maybe we should acknowledge what's going on, admit that this is something rare and special."

I nod slowly, agreeing with her. "It is. This had been incredible and you're... well, you're very special to me." My lips pull into a smile because I see where she's heading now. "So you think we should give this a name? As in dating?"

"Yeah. We can still date, no matter how far apart we live and it's not like we're short of funds to fly back and forth to see each other." Syd shrugs. "I'd like you to be my girlfriend."

"Girlfriend," I say, more to myself, because the word needs a little getting used to. A career-driven woman like me has a husband, or a partner, not a girlfriend. Yet, that simple word fills me with joy and makes me giddy with excitement, like I'm seventeen years old all over again. I haven't been my usual self in the past two days; to-the-point, serious and no-nonsense, but rather dreamy and passionate. Or maybe I'm wrong and I've been exactly that: myself. Maybe I've found a part of me that was lost because I feel so at ease with her. I'm not pretending to be someone I'm not and I'm not trying to impress her. Neither is she, and that gives me hope that this might actually be the start of something beautiful.

"Are you uncomfortable with giving this a name?" Syd asks, sensing my internal back-and-forth. "Because we don't have to."

"No, I'm not uncomfortable." I sit right up and lean forward, needing to be closer to her. Just having her on the other side of the tub seems too far away now, and I miss her warmth. "I like girlfriend. Girlfriend is good."

Syd looks both happy and relieved as she makes a twirling gesture with her finger, suggesting that I turn around. When I sink back against her body, I know this is right. I want to be with her, see where this takes us. I'm not exactly a romantic at heart, but with Syd, I feel like I'm living in a dream and I don't want to wake up. She wraps her arms around me and buries her face in my neck, inhaling deeply against my skin. "Good. Then we'll see each other again very soon." She runs her fingertips over my breasts, making me shiver. "So don't think about goodbyes right now. Think about all the fun stuff we can do before the morning comes."

22

My hands are tied behind me, and Syd's arm around my waist is holding me up as my legs feel like they're going to give way underneath me. Her other hand is holding the tie of the red, silk fabric around my wrists, pulling me back against her. I'm facing myself in the bathroom mirror, watching her take me from behind. She's wearing her robe and her strap-on, pounding into me. It's one of the most erotic and sinful sights I've ever witnessed, and I can hardly believe this is me. My breasts are bouncing and my skin is gleaming with sweat. My hair is a wild tumble, my eyes burning with hunger and my red and swollen mouth is sore from hours of kissing. Intoxicated by arousal, I meet her gaze and hold my breath as she suddenly stops. My heartbeat accelerates, knowing what's coming.

She lets go of my waist, grabs the vibrator from the sink in front of me and places it against my clit, pushing down on it, forcing my hips back as she stays still inside me. Watching me closely, she smiles as I thrash in her grip and let out a loud, throaty moan.

The sweet tightening in my core is growing stronger and I need her to let me come this time or I might lose it. She's been teasing me relentlessly, withholding me from my orgasm three times already and I'm praying that now is the moment she'll stop the sweet torture and let me implode. Just as I'm about to tip over the edge, she throws the device back into the sink and remains still, stroking my breasts and biting my earlobe. Her heavy breathing in my ear tells me she's using all her willpower not to continue and chase release herself. I try to push back against the shaft, but she stops me and holds me still, waiting until my imminent orgasm subsides. My behind is glowing, her hand marks undoubtedly visible on my skin from earlier. I want her marks there, and I want the hickeys on my neck. They'll be a reminder of her when I get home tomorrow, something to remember her by when I miss her.

"Please," I say, shooting her a begging look. "Please fuck me and make me come."

Dark clouds seem to skitter over Syd's pale eyes, and I think my plea has taken away her last restraint as she slowly pulls out and then eases into me again. I suck in a breath through clenched teeth when she holds my arms behind me, yanks at the silken ties and starts fucking me relentlessly. The delicious feeling that envelops me every time she thrusts inside me makes me close my eyes, and everything cuts to white noise.

"Look at me," I hear her say, and I open my eyes again to watch her. She loses her rhythm as her climax approaches but keeps her gaze fixed on me. I can't wait any longer and allow myself to combust. Her hips push hard into my behind as my pussy clenches around the shaft and then she lets out the most beautiful cry that is so pure, it almost takes me out of the moment. Her arms wrap around me and she pulls me close against her, burying her face in my hair, shaking and breathing fast. I can still feel her hips jerking against me when she finally lets go and unties my hands.

Together, we drop to the cold, tiled floor because right now, neither of us has the energy to take another step. Syd opens her robe and pulls me into it, and as I align myself with her warm body, we fall into a tender kiss. Her hands are on my cheeks and her lips brush lightly over mine, barely touching as we breathe in each other's air. I don't know why, but I feel like crying and before I know it, a tear runs down my cheek.

"Hey, are you okay?" Syd whispers before kissing it away.

I nod. "Yeah, I'm fine. I don't know what's happening to me, I just feel so..." I swallow hard. "Happy, I guess... and calm."

"That makes sense." Syd gives me a sweet smile. "You needed this."

"I did," I admit. "I needed you, I think." I'm not sure if that statement scares her, but she doesn't seem fazed.

"I needed you too," she admits. "And I'm so glad you're here."

I'm wrapped up in Syd's robe and she's wearing sweatpants and a T-shirt as we drink tea on her balcony with a blanket around us. I'm sitting on her lap because the chair on the other side of the table seemed too far away, and I want to be close to her while I still can. Below us, the street is deserted as a storm has hit the city. Thunder is rumbling in the background and now and then, lightning strikes, lighting up her beautiful face. I could look at her forever and never get tired of it.

"When did you know you liked women?" I ask.

"I always knew," Syd says, as if that should make perfect sense to me. "I had my first real crush on a girl when I was twelve and ever since, I never doubted my sexuality." She looks at me and grins. "When did you know you liked women?"

I know it's a joke, but I still answer. "Probably the first time I saw your picture." Licking my lips, I stare at her luscious mouth that has been all over my body by now. "I honestly couldn't stop looking at it."

Syd puts down her tea and squeezes me. We're the total cliché of two new lovers who can't get enough of each other; excited, giddy, tactile, constantly on the brink of arousal. "I wanted you from the first time I saw your picture too." Her smile fades, and she looks at me intently. "Would you have a problem with being gay?"

"No..." I shrug. "It just is what it is and that's fine. If anything, I'm grateful that I discovered this about myself, even though I'm a little late to the party and I feel like I've wasted years not knowing how good it could be with a woman." I pause as my mind wanders. "But if I'd known sooner, I probably wouldn't have met you."

"That's true. And that would be a shame now, wouldn't it?" She arches a brow and studies me as I hesitate. "Is there anything else you wanted to ask?"

"Yeah..." I purse my lips as I ponder over more things I don't understand. "How did you know you liked to... dominate? Can I say that?"

"You can say that. You can call it anything that feels right." Syd kisses my cheek and shoots me an adoring look as if I'm a toddler who's only just learned how to walk. "It was never an instant thing, more like a growing curiosity. I was drawn to it but didn't experience it personally until I dated an older woman when I was in my early twenties. She wanted me as her submissive, but I discovered that I preferred being on the other side. It's not a lifestyle for me, though. Not like for some people. It's something that I enjoy doing if the opportunity presents itself, but I won't go looking for it. But with the right person it can be very sexy." She brushes a lock of hair behind my ear and cups my cheek. "I like normal sex too; it's raw and carnal, and it can be beautifully intimate, life-changing even. But sometimes, I like to play. It's the waiting, the anticipation, the patience from both sides." She gives me a playful smile. "And I love to tease, to build tension. Knowing I can make someone explode like you did tonight is both powerful and humbling at the same time. So, I guess for me, it's like with food. Today I might feel like going for an indulgent meal in a fine dining restaurant and tomorrow I might just want to devour a burger."

I laugh at that comparison, even though it makes perfect sense. "I get that. Sometimes you're Sydney Heller and sometimes you're Sadie London."

"Exactly." She tilts her head and traces my neck to my collarbone, then farther down until her fingers settle between my breasts. "It's natural with you, like I know what you want, and you know what I want."

Our conversation is interrupted by a loud crash of thunder and then the rain starts pouring down. I like how it changes the scent in the air, and the sound it makes as it splashes against the ivy on the railings. The rain is blowing into the sheltered balcony, but I don't mind—the sensation invigorating as it hits my face. Neither does Syd, as she closes her eyes and raises her gaze skyward. Droplets trickle down her cheeks, her nose and her chin, caressing her beautiful features. I simply can't stop looking at her and when the droplets settle above her upper lip, I lean in and lick them away. My action stirs her back into the present, and she kisses me with such conviction that everything around me fades. The noise of the thunder and the rain on my skin... even the cold is gone as the robe slips off my shoulder and I turn to deepen the kiss.

23

A layer of condensation settles on the windows after a good thirty minutes of making out in the car. Syd's lips feel heavenly on mine as I straddle her in the driver's seat, rolling my hips on her lap while our tongues engage in a passionate dance. The darkness and privacy of the airport parking lot is tempting, but we have to be careful not to take it too far as we'll never get out of here.

Reluctantly, I pull away because my flight leaves in an hour and this is cutting it really fine. "I have to go."

"I know." My breath quickens again as Syd's hands disappear under my dress and make their way up my thighs. Although I know we don't have time for this, I can't resist her touch. Time is so precious now, and any moment I can steal with her is one that I'll take. A hand snakes up around my waist, then settles firmly on my back while her other moves down to my pussy, rubbing me hard. I throw my head back and let out a whimper, then moan softly as she pulls the fabric of my drenched panties to the side and slips two fingers inside me. She locks her eyes with mine and shoots me a flirty smile as she curls them. "But this will only take two minutes."

I nod and look at her through hazy eyes, then kiss her again as I start riding her fingers. I know for a fact it won't take longer than two minutes, because it's not the first time she's done this to me.

"I want to feel you tighten around my fingers one more time, see the pleasure coursing through you. It's so incredibly beautiful to watch," Syd mumbles against my mouth. "And I want you to feel where I've been when you're on that flight, so you'll think of me."

There's no doubt I'll think of her. Syd has a way with words that drive me wild. My pace quickens, and I'm moving faster, chasing release. "Yes..." I look at her, wanting her to see what she does to me, how good she makes me feel. She touches the spot that always sends me over the edge, and it doesn't fail to amaze me how well she knows my body. But I know hers too, by now. Every inch of skin, each beauty mark, all her erogenous zones. I know a blush creeps onto her neck when I slide my hands under her top, and I know exactly how she'll respond if I breathe into her ear; goose bumps, a shiver, her breath hitching... I intuitively know where she wants to be touched and what she likes, the same way she responds to my needs. It's fluid, like we're tuned in to the same wavelength, effortlessly communicating our desires without speaking. As the waves of my orgasm crash through me, I kiss her like it's the last thing I'll ever do. I take everything in; the way her lips feel, her tongue, her whimpers, her breath, her smell and the way she holds me as I shake in her arms, afraid to forget the important things a video call can't capture. Letting out a deep sigh, I sit back and shiver when she pulls out of me. "Walk with me?"

. . .

W hen we're inside the terminal she lets go of my hand and pulls me in, running a hand through my hair. I wrap my arms around her neck and breathe in her scent one more time. The past two days have changed my life forever, and whatever happens between us, I'll always cherish this. If it was up to me, we'd continue to see each other but being so far away, I'm not sure how it will turn out, even though she says she'll visit. Some people go by 'out of sight, out of mind', and I used to be like that myself. With Syd though, I know I won't forget her, and if I have to, it will be very hard to get over her. I feel so much more for her than I've felt for previous lovers. Passion, lust, respect, admiration, adoration... I'm still clutching onto her and miss her already.

"I had no idea this was going to be so hard," I say, surprising myself with my honesty. "Thank you, it's been amazing." I fight back the tears because I know it's ridiculous to cry after the short amount of time that we've actually spent in each other's presence, but I fail and a tear trickles down my cheek when I let go.

"It has been amazing. I'm going to miss you so much." Syd cups my cheek, brushes the tear away with her thumb and kisses me softly. If I'm not mistaken, she seems a little emotional herself, and there's a tremor to her voice when she continues. "I'll see you very soon, okay? I'll let you know once I've booked my flight."

I nod and tear myself away from her. "I'll see you online, then?"

She gives me a sweet smile and backs off, letting me go. "Yeah, I'll see you online." I turn and watch as she walks away—boyishly handsome and swaying her hips—wondering if I'll ever see her again.

24

By the time I've boarded I'm a bundle of nerves, and I appreciate the privacy of the walls around my little business class cabin. Knowing she's driving back home, and that as soon as we take off I'll be on my way to a different time zone again, is a thought I'd rather not entertain. Being away from her makes me uncomfortable, and I desperately try to hang onto the feeling of our last hug. How she held me, kissed me, looked at me... This was only supposed to be a casual meet up; for me to satisfy my curiosity, and maybe get some answers, and I can only assume her intentions were the same. But now, everything is muddled and I'm not sure how I feel. All I know is that it has genuinely upset me to leave her and that I must be crazy if I feel this after only two nights. I couldn't have known she'd be even more amazing in real life, and I couldn't have known our chemistry would be through the roof, or that she'd bring out a side to me I didn't know I had, like she knew me better than myself.

As soon as we're in the air, I recline my comfortable chair, take off my heels and stretch my legs out in front of me. The hostess offers me a glass of Champagne and I gladly accept, hoping it will release some of the tension and restlessness inside me.

Looking for distraction, I reach for the magazines in the stand behind the mini bar and absentmindedly flick through them, already wondering what she's doing. I imagine her visiting me in LA, showing her my favorite hangouts. Although I haven't been to the beach in years, that's the first thing that springs to mind. Maybe I just want to see her in a bikini, or maybe I'm longing for a change. Living in Santa Monica, it's a crime how little time I spend enjoying the beach while it's practically a stone's throw from my apartment. I close my eyes and see us on loungers, sipping cocktails while we enjoy the view, then wading out into the ocean until we're almost immersed, holding each other as we're bobbing on the waves. Suddenly, I can't think of anything better than being in the water with her. Our near-naked bodies pressed together, our limbs tangled, making out until we're too turned on to continue. Rushing home, ravaging each other in the shower, then on the bed, or on the dining table...

As I sip my Champagne and let my imagination run free, other scenes enter my mind and they're not just sexual. I think about us drinking coffee together on my balcony in the mornings, reading the newspaper while she writes, occasionally talking and sharing a kiss. Introducing her to my friends... maybe even my family. Curiously, it's the mundane things that I long for, the idea of being together in everyday life. How did I get in so deep so fast? Was it the talking, the sex? The talking wasn't just talking, and the sex wasn't just sex. It was a journey, an exploration of each other, as well as ourselves... I trusted her wholeheartedly and whatever happens between us, I know I always will.

Memories keep me entertained throughout the flight, visions of her walking around the bed with the crop in her hand making me squirm in my seat. Syd's my ultimate fantasy, there's no point in denying that. I knew her sexual predilections—or should I say Sadie London's—through reading her books, and as a result she soon discovered mine. It's a simple explanation, yet it doesn't justify the powerful energy between us that was both instant online and in real life. Frankly, the whole situation is hard to get my head around. Chemistry happens when people are face to face, but in our case, it happened way before that. I swallow away my train of thought by finishing my Champagne because it only brings up more questions I'm not able to answer.

After lunch I connect to the airline's Wi-Fi, hoping work might distract me but I soon realize I'm opening my Messenger app instead. I'm so used to checking it throughout the day, hoping Syd will be online, that it always comes first these days, and when the green light springs on, my heart jumps. Even though I've only just seen her, my reaction to the simple change of color is astounding.

'You have Wi-Fi...' she types.

'I do. I'm in business.' I add a wink emoji.

'Of course you are .' Then she adds: *'I miss you already. Can I have a picture?'*

I blush and attempt to take a selfie. It's not like anyone can see me in here but the fact that she misses me puts a silly grin on my face, so I check to make sure there are no flight attendants walking past. It's quiet in the aisle and I'm guessing most passengers are taking an after-lunch nap. I send the shot, then type: *'Miss you too. Now where's my picture?'* I want to call her but it's too quiet in here to do that.

'God, you're beautiful,' is her reply.

I wait, and my patience is rewarded when a picture of

her face fills both my screen and my heart. *'And you're hot.'* Syd's more than hot. She's got this incredibly irresistible boyish smile and her glacial blue eyes under sharp, dark eyebrows are spirited and mysterious, sometimes carrying a hint of devilry.

Another message comes in and I reluctantly click the picture away, saving it for later.

'I'm booking my flight. Is next month okay for you?' She adds: *'I know you'll have to work, but so do I, so I'll keep myself busy.'*

'Yes, next month is perfect!' I immediately reply. My excitement goes through the roof, knowing this is happening. She really is coming. *'How long for?'*

'A week? I can always keep my options open and stay longer if you want me to.'

'You know I want you to.' My fingers tremble as I type. *'Stay as long as you can.'* I wait for a reply and it seems to take forever. Finally, a message comes back.

'Booked . Have to go to the studio now. Talk to you later?'

'Absolutely. Bye. X'

'Bye. X'

I sit back and let out a deep sigh, then raise my hand to order another glass of Champagne because I feel like I've just won the jackpot.

25

"Tell me, how was it?" Ellen tastes the wine and nods to the waiter, allowing him to fill our glasses. "You've totally neglected me over the past week, so I need you to talk."

We're having Sunday brunch in a vineyard in Malibu. It's located a couple of miles inland and looks out over a long stretch of vines and green hills. I love coming here because the service is excellent and most of the customers are true wine lovers, who are not here to brag, but rather to enjoy the vineyard's signature white Cabernet Sauvignon and their great, fresh food.

"I'm sorry," I say, feeling bad for ignoring her text messages. "It's been busy at work and I've spent my nights talking to Syd."

"Well, Syd's not here and now it's time for me, so shoot." Ellen sits back and tilts her head, regarding me. "You look different. Kind of girlie; all sweet and innocent." She nods to my white cotton top. "What happened to the black?"

"Nothing, it's just warm today."

She arches a brow. "Yeah right. And that blush on your cheeks, is that from the heat too?"

I smile and think about what to say for a moment, because it's hard to find the words to describe how I feel. Apart from the fact that I'm terribly distracted and constantly turned on, I've found myself passing the week in a dreamy haze. I managed to function at work, but only just, and as the afternoons progressed, the butterflies in my stomach multiplied in anticipation of my daily call with Syd. "It was amazing," I finally say, unable to come up with anything better.

"What was amazing? The sex or Syd?" Ellen's eyes widen in excitement.

"Yes, the sex was mind-blowing." I pause. "But Syd was amazing too." God, I love saying her name out loud and I feel myself blushing as it rolls off my tongue. I don't go into detail about the sex, it's something sacred, between me and her.

"So, sounds like you guys had a special connection? In and out of bed?"

"Yeah. It was the strangest thing; I felt like I really got to know her, and we just clicked on all levels." Shaking my head, I take a sip of my wine. "That probably sounds silly to you because I was only there for two nights..."

"That does sound quite intense for such a short visit. So, are you officially into women now?"

"I guess so. I don't see myself in bed with a man ever again, but to be completely honest with you, I don't see myself having sex with another woman either. I just want her."

"Jesus. You're so into her, it's almost sickening." Ellen pauses and grins. "Are you in love with Syd?"

I shrug, unsure of anything apart from the fact that I

miss her and want to be with her all the time. "Have you ever felt so close to someone that you feel like you can't live without them?"

"Yeah, I feel that way about you," Ellen jokes. "And I was kind of hoping it was mutual."

I roll my eyes and laugh. "I love you too, Ellen, but you know very well what I mean."

"Yeah, I do, actually." Ellen sits back, and her expression turns serious as my question circulates in her mind. "I've felt that way about someone, but only once." She sighs. "Our mailman when I still lived with David…"

"You're joking, right?" I chuckle and try not to imagine Ellen dressed in a negligée, luring in the mailman with a false promise of coffee.

"No, I'm not. We were the last house on his round, and I was often out in the front yard when he dropped the mail over. At first, it was just 'good morning', and 'how are you', but soon enough, we started talking more and then one day I invited him in for a coffee. His name was Steve Jordan…" Her voice trails away as she says his name. "We developed some kind of weird friendship. Nothing ever happened; he was married too, but there was always this tension between us and later on, I think we both knew that we really liked each other. I couldn't wait for him to show up and he would rush his rounds, so he had more time to spend with me. But then I got divorced, moved away and I never saw him again. It just felt wrong to contact him because he was married but I cried about him, Val. I cried about him a lot. Everyone thought I was devastated by my divorce, but all my tears were a result of losing the mailman." She takes a sip of her wine and pauses when the waiter brings over our scrambled eggs and smoked salmon. "I'm over it now, but boy that was a hard time."

"I'm sorry, I had no idea."

"I never really told anyone. People would assume I was just a desperate divorcée with a stupid crush." She shrugs. "But when I think about it, I can't stop wondering if he was the one, you know? If there's only one person out there for each of us and if I missed my chance..."

"Do you believe that?" I sip my coffee and spear a slice of salmon onto my fork. "Do you believe there's only one person out there who you're meant to be with?" I think of the coincidences that have happened to me over the past month. Ordering the wrong book, joining a book club, meeting Syd—who I feel an overwhelming passionate connection with—and then finding out she was the author of the books I'd been reading.

"I don't know," Ellen says. "Whether she's 'the one' or not, if you really feel this strongly about her, you're going to have to make an effort to keep her, because Quebec is not around the corner." She pulls a sour face as she utters the word 'Quebec', making us both laugh and lightening the mood.

26

The door buzzer makes me shoot up from the couch, and my heart races, knowing she's here. I've been waiting for the past three hours because Syd was delayed and told me she'd get a cab to my place as she wasn't sure how long it was going to take. As a result, I paced around the house so much that I'm pretty sure I damaged the floor before I finally forced myself to sit down with a glass of scotch to settle my nerves. Rushing over to the mirror in the hallway, I check how I look before I press the intercom button to let her in. After getting changed five times, I decided it made no sense being dressed and opted for my silk robe instead. Syd's seen it so many times in our video calls that it's only fair she gets to take it off in person.

When I open the door, I have no time to take her in or process our reunion because she slams it shut and pushes me against the wall. Her hips are grinding into me, her hands moving through my hair as she kisses me like it's all she's been thinking about over the past few weeks. Her lips part and we sink into an all-consuming kiss, moaning as we let our hands roam freely. She pulls at the tie and opens my robe, never taking her mouth off mine. Her hands slide around my waist, over my back and then to the front again, cupping my breasts as she leans into me.

I didn't even see what she was wearing when she came in, and I'm glad to feel it's a shirt so I can undo the buttons without breaking the kiss. My fingers feel clumsy as I fumble to open them, impatient to feel her skin against mine. Her own unique scent is permeating the air, the light smell of soap and a hint of cologne driving me wild. It's been five long weeks since I last saw her, and every day I've longed for her more.

Syd sighs deeply when I pull her shirt off and our bodies finally connect again. She feels warm and soft like I remember, her abs hard against my belly as she pulls out of the kiss and walks me backward through the hallway, and into the kitchen. Our eyes meet for the first time and electricity sparks between us. Just one look is enough to make my heart skip a beat. I'd almost forgotten how incredibly attractive she was, how her picture or her face on video doesn't even come close to the sexual energy she gives off in person. When she smiles at me, I'm totally lost and putty in her hands.

"I want to fuck you so badly it hurts," she murmurs in a low voice, looking me up and down. My robe is hanging open and I'm naked underneath, completely waxed, knowing how much this turns her on. She scans the space and her eyes settle on the kitchen island.

My breath hitches at her words and, knowing what she's thinking, a flash of heat hits my core. "Then fuck me," I whisper, taking another step back until I hit the side of the big cooking island. I've actually never used it before. Since I rarely cook, I regretted spending so much money on an industrial designer kitchen, but now I'm thinking it was totally worth it after all.

Syd lifts me onto the island, and I crawl back when she climbs on it too, pushing a pile of paperwork to the floor to clear the space. Her gorgeous body is still covered by a sports bra and her jeans, and she's still got her sneakers on. It arouses me that she wants me so badly she hasn't even gone through the effort of taking them off. Like a predator, she goes straight for the kill and wastes no time with foreplay. Her biceps flex as she lowers herself on top of me, then kisses me deeply while she runs a hand between my legs and cups my pussy, squeezing me hard. It feels so good and I thrust my hips against her, then cry out when she enters me and fills me up with two fingers. My reaction makes her mouth pull into a smile against mine and she pushes further, while her other hand grabs my wrists and pins them above my head. A deep, guttural groan passes my lips, and it encourages her to start fucking me, fast and hard.

"Come for me, Val." Syd speaks my language, knows what I need. It's like her command fires off a spark and only seconds later, I tense up and hold my breath, almost losing it when she sucks my tongue into her mouth while flicking her thumb over my clit. I dissolve into pleasure as shockwaves ripple through me, my body a raw synapse of twitches that fan out like a stone that's been dropped in water. She continues to sink into me, over and over until I have nothing left and I'm splintered and spent.

Looking up at her, I wiggle my hand loose and run my fingers through her short hair, then cup her face. I still can't believe she's actually here, and that I can touch her, breathe the same air, smell her, hear her whisper in my ear. She's stunning, and I want her out of her clothes so that I can fully immerse myself in her. "Do you want to see my bedroom?"

Syd's eyes darken and she gets off the counter before helping me off too. Her gaze roams over my open kitchen and living space, taking in the ultra-modern interior and luxurious fittings and furniture. "If it's anything like this, then I definitely want to see your bedroom..."

"Come here," I say, unbuttoning her jeans. I pull them down and she steps out of them. The carnal look in her eyes has faded, replaced by a softness, something much more vulnerable now. It almost brings a lump to my throat as I trace her waist and her hips, marveling at how good it feels to have my hands on her again. I pull her sports bra over her head, slide down her panties and slip my robe to the floor so that we're both fully naked. With her clothes, her façade has dropped too. The dominance has evaporated, and she radiates a warmth and tenderness that makes me want her even more.

We're standing on the thick, silk rug in my bedroom, that is indeed a reflection of the rest of my apartment. It's also my favorite room. My interior designer spent a lot of time and effort on creating a haven for me where I can switch off after a hard day's work. It's minimalist and mostly white, yet the mixture of fabrics and textures used still gives it a sense of coziness.

In front of the sliding glass doors, leading onto the balcony that offers fantastic views of the ocean, is a wooden platform with a built-in Jacuzzi, big enough to hold four. I love to open my doors in the morning and take a bath while I watch the sun come up. There are scented candles on the nightstands, and more candles on the coffee table in the seating area where a 2-seater designer couch and two armchairs I never use, smarten up the room. The custom-made Japanese king-size bed is placed against the wall in the middle of the room, and no one but me has been in it, since I moved in. It's perfect in every way apart from one thing: there are no bedposts—nothing for me to be tied to. For now though, that is not my concern as I just want to be close to her and make her feel good.

"I want you," I whisper, taking her hand and pulling her onto the bed. My heart swells as I cup her face and hear her breath hitch before I kiss her. She tugs me closer and softly bites my bottom lip, then deepens the kiss as she lets her tongue swirl around mine. We're melting together, floating into bliss as our bodies become one. This is right, she's who I'm meant to be with; I've never been surer of anything.

I pull out of the kiss and trace my lips down her neck, drawing a moan from her mouth. My hands are everywhere and so are hers. I love her breasts and take a nipple into my mouth, then draw it out along the length of my tongue until she's shifting under me, jerking her hips up. I move farther back and sigh as I spread my legs, lower myself onto her and grind into her pussy. It drives her insane; I can tell by her breathing and her hazy eyes. Guttural noises come from deep within her, and she has trouble lying still. "Is that good?" I ask, rubbing myself harder against her glistening folds. She's wet and swollen, shaking with need. I reach between us and part her lips. The contact makes me quiver as it's so raw and intense, and even though she's just fucked me roughly on the kitchen island only five minutes ago, I'm already close again.

"So good..." Her hands reach for my thighs, her nails digging into my flesh as she continues. "Don't stop, Val. What you're doing is incredible..."

I arch my back and steady my hands on her calves behind me, continuing the slow and sensual pace that is about to send us both to greater heights. Syd lets out a loud groan and I let go too, pushing into her as we climax. She looks into my eyes and takes my hands, lacing our fingers together. When I fall forward and bury my face in her neck, she holds me so tight that I can barely breathe. I squeeze our hands together and stretch my legs out, covering her delicious body with my own. Her abs tense against my belly as aftershocks ripple through her and the lowering sun warms my behind and highlights her face in the most beautiful way. She looks like a dream, but she's very, very real and I can honestly say that nothing could make this moment any better.

27

I feel a breeze on my skin as I wake up and smile when I see Syd sitting on my bedroom balcony, drinking coffee as she takes in the view. The sliding doors are wide open, filling the room with the scent of the ocean. My linen curtains are blowing into the room and the leaves of the large bunches of white lilies on the nightstands and the coffee table are rustling in the soft gusts of wind. I started buying lilies after I came back from Quebec, craving a reminder. With Syd being here, the whole vibe of my modern bedroom has changed, as if her presence covers everything in a romantic filter. I can smell coffee too, and when I sit up to look at the clock on my nightstand, I see she's made me an espresso.

"Good morning, princess," she says, turning to me when she hears me stir. "I've been exploring your palace and made myself a coffee, hope you don't mind." She's wearing boy shorts and a white tank top and looks super sexy with her legs stretched out on another chair as she soaks up the sun.

"Good morning." I'm aware of my goofy grin but unable

to hide my excitement as I take a sip of the fresh brew and lock my eyes with hers. "Of course I don't mind." I hold up my cup. "And thank you."

"You're welcome." She shoots me a flirty look. "You look gorgeous when you're sleeping, but I didn't want to creep you out by staring at you in bed, so I came out here."

I laugh and wrap my naked body in the white cotton sheets, then walk out onto the balcony to join her with my coffee in hand. When I lean over to kiss her, she pulls me onto her lap and wraps her arms around me. "I like having you here." I kiss her softly, but Syd is not one for subtle, and she runs her hands through my hair, pulls me closer and deepens the kiss. By the time we pull apart I'm dizzy and aroused, and we both laugh when we realize the sheets have dropped, putting me on full display for the beach goers. I quickly pick it up to cover my modesty and let out a deep sigh of contentment as I lean into her.

"And I like being here." Syd studies me, licking her lips. I love how she's never entirely satisfied, always looking at me as if she's ready to ravish me, even after last night. "I knew you were a big shot, but I didn't think you'd live in a place like this." She shrugs. "Not that it makes a difference to me; I just want you and I would have been happy with you living in an RV as long as I got to fuck you... but you've got a good thing going on here, Val."

I feel myself blush, knowing it must look a little excessive. "I know. I'm grateful for everything I have, but I must admit that I've never appreciated my kitchen and my bedroom as much as I did last night."

Now it's Syd's turn to laugh, and a mischievous twinkle appears in her eyes as she sneaks a hand under the sheet and cups my breast. "It's a big penthouse, and I'm sure you'll have a newfound appreciation for a lot of other rooms and places soon."

"Oh yeah? Where do you suggest we start?" A shiver runs down my spine as she pulls my hair to one side and bites my earlobe.

"Well, for starters..." Syd whispers in my ear, "The Jacuzzi is high on my list." She pauses, placing hot kisses down to the base of my neck. "And I like the shower behind your bed." Her lips continue over my shoulder while her thumb brushes over my nipple, making me crave her even more. "And the dining room table of course, the couch, the bathroom and the guest bedroom..." She chuckles. "But right now, I think we should start with your balcony, seeing as it's such a lovely, sunny day."

Her words make me quiver, and I take in a quick breath as her hand moves down, between my thighs. "I can't," I say, delirious with lust but conscious of the downstairs neighbors. "Someone will hear us... or see us." I didn't care as much in Quebec as I didn't think I'd come back there, but in this building, everyone knows me. It's Sunday and I can hear them one and two floors below. The Richardsons are cooing at their newly adopted baby, and Mrs. Walters is talking on the phone as usual, laughing loudly at her own jokes.

Syd shakes her head, clearly not bothered by our lack of privacy. "Then you'll just have to be very quiet and act like you're simply drinking your coffee on my lap while I make you come. Can you do that?"

"I don't know," I say honestly. Being quiet is not my strong point when it involves her, but her teasing smile is so charming that I couldn't resist her even if I wanted to. My heart is racing but I don't protest as her fingers have found my clit and are doing something only Syd can do. "Yes," I whisper, and try my best not to moan when she starts making delicious circles with her middle and index finger, putting pressure where I need it most.

"Yeah?" Syd's fingers move faster, driving me insane. Clinging onto the sheet so it won't drop again, I lean back against her and close my eyes, giving in to the tightness that builds in my core. My gasp is stifled by her hand on my mouth, as she continues her quest to make me come fast and hard.

"Shhh..." she whispers in my ear when she feels me tense up. "Be quiet."

I nod, but when my climax rolls over me, a guttural groan escapes my lips anyway, followed by a loud 'fuck!' I'm shaking and need time to compose myself, but I already hear the shuffling of Mrs. Walters shoes on her balcony.

"Valerie?" I shake my head and laugh when she yells my name. "Are you alright, dear?"

"Yes, I'm fine, thank you." My voice sounds shaky as I wrap the sheet tight around me and walk over to the balcony railing to meet her curious stare. "I just bashed my toe, that's all."

"Sounded like you were in pain." Mrs. Walters looks at the sheet that covers me and runs a hand through her gray perm. She's only ever seen me dressed in my black suits and I think she's shocked to learn I was still in bed at 9 am. I hear Syd chuckle behind me and shoot her a playful warning look over my shoulder. "I apologize," Mrs. Walters continues. "I didn't realize you had company."

"That's okay," I say, thinking there's no point in denying it as she's going to see Syd at some point. The highly conservative older woman will have a field day when she finds out what's going on but it's none of her business and I'm going to do whatever I want in my palace, as Syd calls it. "Well, I'd better take a look at my toe. Have a good day, Mrs. Walters." When I turn around, Syd has gotten up from her chair and she scoops me up in her arms. I shriek and laugh out loud as she carries me into the bedroom and drops me on the bed. Staring up at her with an adoring look in my eyes, I tug at her top. "Take that off please. I want to make love to you."

28

"Are you hungry?" I squeeze Syd's hand as we walk along Santa Monica Boulevard. After spending most of our Sunday in bed, I've shown her my favorite places, at least the ones within walking distance, before we continued our walk on the beach, barefoot, and watched the sunset together. Contrary to what I suspected, nothing about Syd being here is awkward, and I feel relaxed and at ease by her side. "I'd take you to The Vineyard but it's a little farther out and I don't feel like driving today, so maybe we could go somewhere local for food?"

Syd smiles as she pulls me in and wraps her arm around me. "Sure. Do you have a favorite restaurant?"

"Not around here." I hesitate as I glance to the left. "There's this place a few blocks down, but I haven't been there in a while."

"Then let's go there."

"Yeah..." I'm not sure why I thought of that particular restaurant as I used to go there with Brian. *Capri* has an amazing food and wine list, but I haven't been back since my divorce. Besides worrying about running into Brian, it just didn't feel right, too many memories attached to a time in my life I was trying to forget, I suppose. But as I walk here with Syd, I find myself not caring about any of that. The chance of Brian being there is slim, and I'm craving the grilled snapper and Mediterranean salads I used to love. '*Fuck it*,' I think, and before I know it, I've steered us toward *Capri*. Seeing the trees lit-up in their dining yard and hearing the classical guitar music takes me back down memory lane, but not in a bad way.

"This looks nice." Syd says as the hostess welcomes us. She recognizes me and assumes we want to sit inside.

"Outside please," I say, and give her a smile. I applaud her flawless memory, but I want to feel the heat of the night. The guitarist is still sitting on the same chair under the tangerine tree in the middle of the courtyard, playing the same tunes. Nothing has changed, yet everything is different because tonight, *Capri* seems idyllic and incredibly romantic.

When we reach the table and I pull out the chair, Syd sits down on the bench and pats the space next to her. "Come and sit here, princess." She shoots me a flirty wink and I realize how different this situation is. Brian used to sit opposite me, but with Syd, I want to be next to her at all times. We're both very tactile and can't get enough of each other, and I love how she makes me feel attractive and desired, how she always puts me first.

I sink down on the padded bench and can't resist placing a hand on her thigh while I order a bottle of wine. Syd drapes her arm over the backrest, her hand playing with my hair as she studies the menu. I know we look like we're a couple and I don't care, giddy with pride and excitement to be on a date with her. Just like in Quebec, I can see women casting curious glances her way, as if they can somehow sense she's highly sexual. She's wearing jeans and a simple, white T-shirt and I'm dressed down too today, in a short navy and white striped summer dress and white leather sandals. Technically the summer is coming to an end, but it's still warm and clammy. Since meeting Syd, I've loved the sweltering nights. They seem fitting to my feverish mood and the constant passion stirring inside of me, and as I lean into her and make myself comfortable in the crook of her arm, I know I've never been happier.

"They seem to know you pretty well here?" Syd says, twirling a lock of my dark hair around her finger.

"Yeah. I used to come here with Brian," I admit, thinking I might as well get it out of the way. She's probably put two and two together and I don't want to keep anything from her. "But I don't mind being here, I honestly don't." I look up to meet her gaze. "Brian always wanted to sit inside so I've never actually enjoyed this beautiful courtyard. He didn't like heat or wind of dust or... anything really. He also hated insects and birds."

Syd laughs. "Brian sounds a little boring," she jokes. "If you don't mind me saying that."

"No, not at all. He really was boring during our last years together. Or maybe he was just too busy fucking his assistant to do things with me." I pause, reflecting on our time together. "Maybe it was partially my fault too. He clearly didn't feel satisfied in the relationship or he wouldn't have looked for a fling elsewhere."

"Nonsense." Syd kisses my temple. "There's no excuse for bad behavior."

"True, but with him, I never felt how I feel with you and he must have sensed that. But we were friends and that was what hurt the most, the betrayal and the fact that he lied to me. I always admired people who could remain friends after a separation, but in our case, there was too much resentment from my side, I suppose. The cheating and the painful meetings during the divorce procedure was something I just couldn't get over." I shrug. "I haven't spoken to him since and frankly; I feel no need to."

The waitress brings our wine, so we stall our conversation and I turn my attention back to the menu. There's a murmur of voices as a group of men sit down at the reserved table beside us. I don't pay much attention to them, too consumed with the thrilling feel of Syd's body pressed against mine and her hand stroking my shoulder after the waitress has left with our order. A waft of distinct cologne penetrates my senses and I cringe at the smell. There's something about it that I don't like, and I need a moment to figure out why before it hits me. I've made the connection, the all too familiar odor making my stomach drop, and when I turn to look at our neighbors, Brian is sitting there, staring at me. His two friends are looking at us too, and although I've only met them once or twice and don't remember their names, they know exactly who I am.

"Speak of the devil," I whisper, and smile, refusing to let him know I'm dumbfounded. Brian couldn't have looked more stupefied himself and seeing the nervous twitch in his left eyelid makes me feel better. It's crystal clear that Syd's not just a friend and seeing me with a woman is the last thing he would have expected. I curse myself for coming here now, as I should have guessed he was still a regular. Not one for embracing change, Brian likes to stick to what he knows. But it is what it is and there's no point pretending we're strangers as that would be awkward after seventeen years together. "Hi, Brian." I say politely and make no effort to move away from Syd. It pleases me that he's put on some weight and he looks tired, too.

"Hi, Valerie." My name rolls off his tongue clumsily, as if he's almost forgotten it already. "You remember Serge and Nathan?" The reference to his friends seems terribly irrelevant in this situation, but then again, anything we say will sound strange right now. He pulls at his collar and loosens his tie.

"Of course." I give them a wave. "This is Syd."

Syd gives them a charming smile, not in the least taken aback by the presence of my ex-husband. "Nice to meet you."

"Nice to meet you too, Syd." Brian narrows his eyes as he looks from Syd to me and back. "I don't recall ever hearing about you. Are you a new friend of Val's?" I can tell he's dreading the answer and the corners of my mouth tug up as I shake my head. After the initial shock of seeing him again, I'm feeling confident to show him I've moved on, and our unexpected reunion isn't nearly as scary as I thought it would be when I pictured it.

"Actually, Syd's my girlfriend," I say.

"Yeah, I'm the lucky lady." Syd gives him an innocent look as if she has no idea who he is, then places a soft kiss on my temple. Brian's friends, whose names I've already forgotten again, snicker for a moment, then compose themselves, and I note that Brian's face is turning a dark shade of red.

"Right..." Brian clears his throat and looks to the others for help, either at a loss for words or because he's really lost his social skills. "So, you're dating?" he finally asks.

"Uh-huh." I try my best to sound casual. "That's usually what the word 'girlfriend' means. Are you still seeing...?" I pretend that I don't remember his assistant's name, even though I used to look her up on social media daily when I first suspected something was going on between them. "Gladys, was it?"

"Marni," he corrects me and shakes his head. "No, she moved to New York a couple of months ago."

"I'm sorry to hear that." I'm pretty sure he knows I couldn't care less, but it doesn't matter. We're just exchanging formalities and although I'd rather not have Brian here, I won't let him ruin my night.

"It's okay." Brian doesn't look like he's heartbroken over Marni, but he's definitely thrown off his game at seeing me. He fiddles with his gold watch, staring down at the dial as if hoping for it to reveal what to say next. "Well, we were just saying we'd rather sit inside. It's a little warm out here, so you ladies have a good night," he blurts out, ignoring his friends' confused looks. He then stands up and waits for the other two to follow. "It was nice to see you again, Val. You look well."

"Likewise," I lie, and give the group of men a cheerful wave before I turn back to Syd. "Sorry. I didn't expect him to be here... hope it didn't ruin our night."

"Not at all. So that was Brian?" Syd tilts her head and shoots me an amused smile. "I'm glad to see you're over him so that I can have you all to myself."

"Oh, you can tell I'm over him, can you?" I quirk an eyebrow. "Actually, 'over him' is an understatement," I say with a chuckle, and kiss her on the lips. Syd's right; I'm so over Brian, and he must have noticed too. Maybe I was never into him that much in the first place, but one thing I know for sure: I'm very, very much into Syd. The rush I feel when I as much look at her doesn't compare to anything I've ever felt and telling someone else she's mine feels wonderful. "And..." I continue, "In case you didn't notice, I've just introduced you as my girlfriend for the first time."

"I did notice." Syd bites her lip and grins. "Are you okay with that?"

"Yeah, more than okay." I can't seem to stop myself from smiling and neither can Syd. What started as a fantasy is slowly becoming reality and I'm ready to live in the real world, with her.

29

"Are you sure about this?" Syd tilts her head and studies me with an amused smile. "Your co-workers are going to notice."

I laugh, knowing they will and that I'll most likely be the subject of an enormous amount of gossip over the coming months. My wrist is usually covered by my blazer, yet I tend to roll up the sleeves when it gets heated in meetings. It's just something that I do subconsciously, and I'd never be able to avoid it. "I'm sure. Just do it." I'm thinking this is madness, yet it feels so right.

Syd unpacks her tools and lays them out on the dining table in my apartment. She's been here three weeks now and those three weeks have been bliss. She writes on my balcony, or on the beach while I'm at work, and we spend the evenings together; in bed, in town or simply walking along the beach and talking. My co-workers have noticed changes in me, as I'm unusually cheerful at work and often zone out, daydreaming during meetings. Although I've already booked my next flight to see her, I feel sad that's she's leaving tomorrow. She changed her flight to stay longer, but now she has to get back to her studio as her clients' patience is starting to run out.

Having her here has made me re-evaluate my life and I've even been thinking of resigning and starting my own consultancy business, which is something I can do from anywhere. If someone would have told me this six months ago, I'd have laughed in their face, but now, anything to be closer to her seems like a great idea. Syd is open to spending more time here, but I like Quebec, and although Ellen hates me for it, I know I will probably leave LA sometime in the not too distant future.

The tattoo kit I asked her to bring looks daunting, and I shiver as I look at the needles. I hate needles with a passion, but I've taken some painkillers and have poured myself a glass of scotch, although Syd says I'm not allowed to touch my drink until we're done. Unsure of how I'll react once the needle hits my skin, I say: "Maybe you should tie me up for this one."

Syd shakes her head and kisses me sweetly. "I'm not going to tie you up and I'm not going to let you drink. This is a big decision and you need to be sober and one hundred percent sure. So I'm going to ask you again: Are you sure?"

"Yes," I say. "I feel like I'm at a turning point in my life, and I want to remember it." I smile, realizing how content I am right now. Missing pieces have fallen into place, and I'm calmer than ever before because I know who I am. I'm Valerie. I'm not my job, but I like what I do. At work, I like to be in charge, and in the bedroom, I like to submit. I'm a lesbian, in a relationship with the most wonderful and gorgeous woman on this planet. I like to read erotica, go for long walks, and lately, I even like to cook. Sometimes I find myself experimenting in the kitchen for hours, which is something I never thought I'd enjoy. I love sex, art, music and all the things that suddenly make sense when you fall in love with someone. My heart swells when I look at Syd because she's everything to me and I know she deeply cares about me too. It sounds alien coming from me, but now seems like the right time to say the words out loud because I know they're true. "I love you." My voice trembles, and although I'm terrified of her reaction, I need her to know this.

Syd looks at me with so much affection that a lump settles in my throat and several moments pass in silence as she continues to stare at me, processing my words. Then her face lights up as her lips slowly pull into a smile. "I love you too, Val." She stops what she's doing, pulls me onto her lap and wraps her arms around my waist, nuzzling my neck. "I really do."

I put an arm around her neck in return and close my eyes at the warm fuzzy feeling that settles in my core. I can hardly believe how lucky I am to have met her by chance, if there even is such a thing as chance. She knows I really want this to work; I've told her many times over the past few days, but I didn't realize that what I felt for her was love, until now. It's liberating to say it, and to hear her say it back makes me feel whole and connected. Shifting my legs over to one side, I try to wipe the sheepish grin off my face, then offer her my wrist. "Do you want me to move?"

"No, you can stay here." Syd takes my wrist and strokes the spot on the inside where I told her I wanted the tattoo. There's no need for her to ask me if I trust her to do this because trust is one thing we're not short of. While she's been here I've explored my sexual boundaries, surrendered to her daring games in the bedroom, and after each time—when I'm weak and nearly broken—we make love in each other's arms, growing closer each time. "So, I can ink you with anything I want, huh?"

"Anything."

When she switches on the tattoo gun I look away and clench my jaw. "You're quite the wuss for someone who likes to be spanked," she jokes as I breathe in through my teeth and groan in agony. It hurts, but it's not as bad as I thought it would be and she's fast, switching off the machine after only ten minutes. "Done." she says, cleaning my wrist with disinfectant before coating it in a thick layer of Vaseline.

"Can I look?"

"Yes, you can look now." Syd's voice has a rare tremor to it, and I know she's nervous.

When I turn back to look at my wrist, my eyes well up at what I see. In black ink, and in a delicate italic font, she's written: *'Syd's girl'*.

ALSO BY MADELEINE TAYLOR

The Good Girl